# BOOKS BY SUZA KATES

# Rising Storm

## THE SISTERS' GRIMOIRE TRILOGY

## SUZA KATES

ICASM PRESS
SAVANNAH

Published by Icasm Publishing LLC
5710 Ogeechee Rd. Suite 200 #278, Savannah, GA 31405

Library of Congress Cataloging-in-Publication Data

Kates, Suza
Rising Storm / Suza Kates
    p. cm.

ISBN-13:978-1-942318-51-4
ISBN-13:978-1-942318-52-1 (ebook)
I. Title

Printed and bound in the United States of America

10  9  8  7  6  5  4  3  2  1

# Acknowledgements

My heartfelt thanks goes to the team who helps me make to the end every time! Mandi Cranson, Dorothy Beecher, Stella Racicot, Sharyn Cerniglia, Donna Wood, and Alice Yu provide unwavering support and tons of patience! Editing isn't just about commas but also involves cheerleading, counseling, judgment you can trust, and friends you can rely on.

And to the readers, thank you for continuing to read my stories. Your support and kind comments are the always the best reward.

# 1

Night winds raced across the empty parking lot, rustling giant trees thick with summer leaves. Beneath the light of a huge yellow moon, Graysor LeRoux quietly exited his SUV and closed the door with a sof: thud.

For a momer.t he stood still, scanning pockets of shadow around the long stretch of warehouse. No light emitted from the windows. No movement sounded in the immediate area. All was abandoned and silent.

The perfect place for a clandestine meeting.

Ever vigilant, he walked quickly over the cracked cement and scattered gravel of the lot, casting one final look to the flat roof above. Just in case.

He paused at the glass door, peering inside. Somewhere over his head, an owl issued a territorial call. *Hoo-hoo-hoo. Hoo-hoo.* Cautioning Grayson to stay away?

Or warning of something else in the night?

He tossed a glance to the tuft-eared bird, a creature with keen perception and extraordinary night vision. Though not the one that Grayson hunted.

Pulling open the door, he entered a bare room with torn linoleum. The scent of dust and disuse assaulted his nose. Mice droppings littered the floor. He crossed the small lobby and eased through another door, finding himself in a long dark corridor.

A faint glow emanated from the end of the hall, a beacon

drawing him toward the belly of the warehouse.

Once filled with various machines and tools, the building now housed discarded metal parts, grease stains, and the occasional wooden pallet. But Grayson's hard gaze bypassed the garbage, zeroing in on the center of the room, to an out-of-place steel table where two men stood. Portable work lights illuminated their stern faces.

As well as the form on the table, covered by a plain white sheet.

Grayson swore under his breath. He'd known the situation was bad when he'd been called north, all the way to Bangor, Maine, but the presence of a corpse meant things were worse than expected.

That the situation had gone to hell.

Ignoring the stab of worry, he approached with steady steps and cool assessment. If his team had stolen a body, then they'd had good reason. "You made an extraction," he said, more observation than question.

The man on the other side of the table gave a curt nod. "Couldn't be avoided." Tall and red-headed, Finley resembled a Celtic Berserker dressed in black-ops gear. Often the clown of the group and counted on for a joke and a laugh, the grim set of his mouth now reflected Grayson's growing concern.

"We had to get him out of the morgue." Finley's muscles bulged as he clenched his jaw. "Couldn't risk the questions his condition would raise."

"How bad is it?" Grayson asked, coming to a stop beside the table.

"A shit storm." This from Dodge, bald as a billy club and far more deadly. His wiry frame tensed while he studied the victim. He drew a deep breath. "It's just like the old books describe."

*The old books?* Denial roared to life inside Grayson. What was Dodge talking about? He couldn't mean . . .

"Show me," Grayson said, his tone clipped.

Finley shared a glance with Dodge, hesitated, and pulled the sheet down in one quick move.

Grayson studied the corpse, the condition of the body delivering a swift, hard blow that left him stunned. His throat went dry and hot, and his pulse shot into overdrive. Each pounding beat rocked his system.

"Impossible," he uttered, his own voice sounding like a distant echo. His head whirled, searching for alternate explanations as he stared at the cadaver and the evidence it provided. Clear, indisputable proof.

Yet still, his mind revolted.

The dead man was young and in good physical shape, his arms and chest tight with muscle. A prime human specimen. And worthy prey.

He looked barely old enough to buy a beer and, somewhere, Grayson knew, parents were likely grieving a son.

Grayson locked down the thought before compassion could intrude. Emotions only served to distract, and distractions could be deadly.

He curled his right hand into a fist and called forth the mantra. *Even one is too many.* A simple sentence to remind him, to refocus him on his goal. The singular goal shared by Finley, Dodge, and every member of their organization.

This man—this *boy*—was that one too many, but it would do Grayson no good to dwell on the youth or the loss. Instead he directed his attention to the ugly set of holes in the kid's throat. Puncture wounds, large and deep, with decayed flesh rimming the wounds.

"Ever seen anything like it?" Finley asked in a hushed tone.

Grayson only shook his head. *No. Not even close.*

Black lines branched out from the punctures, crawling down the corpse's neck and angling across his torso. They terminated in the upper left quadrant of his chest, where the poison had turned inward, penetrating skin and muscle.

Aiming for the heart.

Across the table from Grayson, Finley held out a finger, tracing the path in the air without touching the cadaver. "The toxin traveled through the flesh and straight into the chest. A quicker route than the veins."

"Different than what we usually see." Dodge scowled as if ready to battle. "More aggressive."

"He had to have been an athlete." Finley stared at the lifeless body. "Big. Strong." He blew out a breath. "If this guy had lived . . ."

"But he didn't," Grayson said. His back corded and strained as he stood immobile, struggling to catch up with his friends, to accept a reality they'd had hours to process. He fell silent again, potential threats and disasters shooting rapid-fire through his brain.

He knew some of the men called him "Ice" behind his back, a nickname earned by his ability to stay calm and straight-faced, no matter the odds. But his methodical nature was currently under siege, battling the effects of pure, blinding shock.

He could hardly come to grips with the truth he faced, but there was no doubt how the man had died. And the significance was staggering.

"Tell me everything," he commanded.

"We got the call in the afternoon," Finley said, crossing his arms. "We set up, and after the morgue cleared out last night, we entered and followed procedure. One look at the body, the discoloration, and the size of those bites—"

"You made the right call," Grayson told him. "The disappearance of a body wouldn't raise nearly as many questions as the discoveries a full autopsy would have yielded."

"With some help from headquarters, we hacked their system." Dodge lifted a shoulder. "Changed the M.E.'s report and wiped some camera feeds. The samples taken were still on site, so we removed those as well." He cleared his throat. "They must have wondered why they couldn't get any blood."

"Anyone hurt during the retrieval?" Grayson's voice fell flat in the vacuous warehouse.

"Only a guard with a headache who will wonder why he fell asleep at his station."

"Good." Grayson gripped the edge of the sheet, paused for one last look, and pulled the coarse material up over the pale, slack face. "We can't lose any time on this. Every hour is critical."

Finley nodded his red head and Dodge grunted agreement.

"Dodge, notify headquarters." Grayson hardened himself, pushing out the last dregs of fear and replacing them with calculation and resolve. "Initiate breach protocol."

Just saying the words locked his lungs again.

As one of the few qualified to give the directive, his authority was the reason he'd been summoned to the site. He'd needed to see the body for himself. He'd had to be sure.

Before activating a plan that had lain dormant for centuries.

"Write down this code." He reeled off a sequence of fourteen numbers, letters, and special characters to Dodge, who then stepped away to make the call.

Grayson spoke to Finley. "I need to see where the body was found."

"The second reason you had to be the one to come up here." Finley's green eyes bore into Grayson. "This calls for a tracker, and we need the best."

Before Grayson could reply, Dodge rejoined them. "It's done," he said gravely. "A local transport team is on the way to take possession of the body. Once the docs down home hear of this, I'm sure they'll be stepping all over each other to start running tests and experiments."

"Let Transport handle it from here then. I want you both with me." Grayson turned and headed back out, the others falling in step beside him. "Bangor's a big city with too many tempting bodies walking around." Bodies filled with hot, fresh blood.

"The body wasn't discovered here," Finley said. "One look at the corpse and authorities sent it to Bangor, to a bigger and more advanced facility."

Grayson let the news roll off his shoulders. "How far do we have to travel?" And how much more time would the trip cost them?

"Not too far. We're headed East. To an island, actually."

Grayson processed the information, deciding this might be their one lucky break. An island meant limited access, fewer escape routes. Which could be good.

Or very, very bad.

"It's near a National Park," Finley said.

"Which means plenty of forest with places to hide." In complete control once again, Grayson opened the door and strode back into the night. "Where is this place?"

The owl's ominous cry drew Finley's attention to the sky. "About an hour's drive," he said. "We're going to Bar Harbor."

# 2

In the attic of her family home, Sami Whiteburn skimmed her fingers down the yellowed page of an ancient book. Not just any book, but an ancestral grimoire. One all but overflowing with magick.

She could only guess when the forest-green leather and fragile paper had originally been crafted, having been passed down through the ages. Still, she treated the tome like the treasure it was, turning time-worn vellum with a soft, gentle touch.

Blowing out a breath, she perused the words. She'd come home tonight for Sunday dinner but had arrived early with another purpose. She'd slipped upstairs to the spacious attic where she'd spent almost two hours scouring the book.

Sure, she'd read the aged pages before, but this time she hoped to stumble across new information, some hint or clue hidden in the script.

Her instincts had recently woken, intuition humming of potential threat. Though she hadn't seen or heard anything out of the norm, she knew better than to ignore this feeling.

Her witchy senses were tingling.

Trouble was coming to Bar Harbor. She was sure of it. Deep, murky trouble of the magickal kind, and odds were it had followed her home.

That's why she'd been searching the book, and why she'd been on edge for the last few days.

She refocused on the page before her. Divided into sections, the grimoire held a plethora of mystical data. Spells, incantations, details on various creatures of lore, and journal entries from all who'd possessed the book. Each segment contained blank pages at the end where each new witch could add their own discoveries.

She and her family had plenty to inscribe from their own Fae-riddled adventures. The most recent had taken them to a farworld known as the Ielonaar Realm, where amidst jagged mountains of stone, her sister Fiona had saved the life of an Iele child.

And their family's enemy had met his brutal end.

Sami sat back in her chair and stretched her arms above her head. Closing her eyes, she inhaled the lemony scent of the wood oil her mother used to clean the attic. She listened as the summer breeze brushed red maple leaves against the high, round window. She tried to embrace familiar things and allow them to comfort.

But in her head, she saw blood. Crimson-splattered rocks and guttural sounds, a beast devouring its prey beneath a sky with twin moons.

She opened her eyes and squeezed the bridge of her nose, telling herself she shouldn't recall Emuirdane's death with such dark satisfaction. But the cruel Iele had taken too much pleasure in tormenting her family. No, she wouldn't miss the sadistic bastard.

But she feared a greater monster had taken his place.

All because of the ring. The one she'd stolen, the one she now kept safe. Like a hidden heartbeat it pulsed in secret, as if trying to get her attention.

Her sisters hadn't mentioned feeling the same way, but they didn't have the same attachment as she did. She'd cast the spell to hide the ring, and she kept it close to her home. She was magickally connected and in close proximity.

And something sinister was brewing. She could *feel* it.

With an exasperated sigh, she pulled the stretchy band from her hair and let reddish-brown curls fall over her shoulders. She'd been staring at the pages for too long, and her head ached from trying to decipher the handwritten lines, some scrawled centuries past.

That and the eye strain told her it was time to quit. The grimoire hadn't provided any great epiphany, and it was better to go down now anyway, before someone started wondering what she was doing up here.

She pivoted in the chair—just in time to see her sisters strolling through the door. She'd almost made a clean escape. *Guess I waited a minute too long.*

"Hey, we're about to eat," Fiona said, her chipper voice not quite disguising the question in her green eyes. "Just wanted to come let you know."

"You came up to let me know about dinner?" Sami asked, crossing her arms and kicking back in the chair she'd been just about to vacate. "Or to check on me?"

"Both," Tate said in her usual brisk manner. As the eldest, she wasn't one to mince words. "You've been up here a while, and it's not like you to take such an intense interest in the grimoire." Countering with her own stubborn crossing of arms, she stared at Sami. "So what's up?"

Typical Tate. Straight to business.

"We wanted to make sure you're okay," Fiona added quickly, a wrinkle forming between her brows. And that was Fee, the baby sister who always worried over other people's feelings.

"I'm fine." Sami lifted her arms and shrugged, playing her own role in the sibling play. She brushed off their concern and pretended nothing was bothering her. "Can't I take a look at the book once in a while?"

"Of course you can," Fiona said. "The Grimoire belongs to all of us."

That was true, but Sami rarely accessed the book, and certainly never stayed bent over the pages for this long. Then again, she'd never felt compelled to by a cold, persistent fear in her chest.

Tate took two steps across the old wooden floor and nailed Sami with a look. "Has something happened with the ring?"

And just like that, the guilt rose up, settling across Sami's shoulders like black ice. "No. I told you nothing was wrong." *Nothing I can put my finger on.*

Standing up, Sami took full advantage of the few inches she had on her older sister and closed the grimoire with a definitive *thump*. "The ring is fine. It's my responsibility, and I told you I'd take care of it."

"It's not only your responsibility, Sami." Tate's stern expression softened. "Any one of us could have grabbed that ring. We *would* have. You just happened to be closest."

Closest to Emuirdane's dismembered hand. With that gruesome image in her mind, Sami worked up a fake smile. "Did I hear Mom say chicken alfredo? I assume that means Fee baked up some seven-grain bread to go with it?"

"Nice diversion," Tate said, thinning her lips. "And yes," she added before Fiona could reply, "all of the above. With peanut-butter brownies for dessert."

"Aw, you didn't." Sami moved to wrap an arm around Tate's shoulders, more than happy to change the topic. Fiona might be the baker in the family, but Tate's brownies were Sami's childhood addiction.

Tate tried to hide her grin. "Yes, but you have to wait until after—"

Sami gave another squeeze and released her to race out the door ahead of her sisters. Before any more talk of the ring could come up.

She quick-stepped down the two flights of stairs and made her way through the Victorian home to the large kitchen. One of her favorite rooms in the house, the central gathering place boasted sage-green walls and a long bank of cream-colored cabinets. The bricks of the arched fireplace had also been painted ivory, but due to the summer weather, no flames snapped within the hearth.

Sami bee-lined for the pan of brownies covered in aluminum foil and cut herself a big square of chocolate-peanut goodness.

"Sami, I swear." Her mother's voice was accompanied by the swat of a towel to Sami's backside. "Almost thirty years old and still sneaking dessert before dinner."

Sami mumbled through a semi-full mouth, "Then aren't I old enough?"

"Your sisters already set the table, so you get to make drinks." Her mother used her hip to nudge Sami out of the way and recovered the pan of brownies.

Sami swallowed and grinned. "I'm on it." She pulled glasses out of a cabinet and filled them with ice. There'd only be eight of them tonight, since Fiona's boyfriend, Ronan, was tying up the last few loose ends in Faerie. He'd led an army known as the Legion, humans serving the Goddess, the Dea Matrona, and sworn to protect an artifact known as the Jeweled Ceffyl.

Since that same artifact was now a live horse prancing freely around pastures, the Legion had been disbanded. And Ronan would soon be home for good.

Knowing what her family liked to drink, Sami filled the glasses and set them around the long wooden table. The tap of a cane announced the arrival of her grandfather, so she looked up. "I made you a water, Granddad. Thought I'd save your Penderyn for later with dessert."

"Hmm." Granddad put a hand to his stomach. "Good idea. Nothing pairs better with chocolate than a good Welsh whiskey."

Sami covered a grimace. Ever since her grandfather had read online about a distillery hosting whiskey and chocolate tours, he'd made the odd combination his new go-to treat.

Right behind Grandad, her uncle Brit walked in with Tate's husband Jack. Both men were tall and wide-shouldered, one dark in coloring and the other fair. Romanian genes ran strong in the Whiteburn family, as evidenced by Brit's black hair.

"I poked my head in and woke Kat," Brit said, speaking of his new bride. After years of hard feelings, the two lovers had reunited, falling for each other all over again and having their nuptials a mere two weeks later. "She'll be down in a minute."

"You could have let her sleep," Sami said, fists going to her hips. "The food would have waited."

"Not an option." Brit shook his head and held out both hands. "The only thing worse than a sleepy Kat is a hungry Kat."

"I heard that," Kat said, slipping between Brit and Jack to take a seat at the table. Her pale blonde hair had been combed, but she still looked drowsy. "I'll let you make up for it by buttering me a slice of Fiona's bread."

"Sure thing." Brit instantly launched into action.

Kat turned to Sami and winked.

"Bad girl," Sami mouthed but still chuckled. Brit insisted on fulfilling Kat's every want or need, and on rare occasion, Kat took full advantage.

"How did you two sleep?" Sami's mother asked, placing a kiss on top of Kat's head before gently patting the not-quite-there baby bump.

Kat's forehead wrinkled. "Okay. I had the most bizarre and vivid dream about—" She stopped herself and slid her gaze to Brit as he handed her the bread. She quickly took a bite, but the ruse was obvious.

"About what?" Sami pressed.

"We're not supposed to talk about it," Kat said, sending an apologetic expression toward Sami's mother.

"Oh." Sami nodded her understanding. Her mother had declared Sunday dinner a Fae-free zone. No talk of Iele, magick jewels, or the potential dangers brewing in other worlds.

"Exceptions can be made," Sami's mother said, "and I don't want you holding things in on my account. I made that rule to stop the three chatter-bugs."

"Oh, you mean me, Tate, and Fiona? The *Daughters of Nadia*?" Sami said with meaning, reminding her mother that their place in the Ceffyl prophecy was because of the magick they'd inherited from her.

"What did the daughters do now?" Fiona entered the kitchen right before Tate. She plopped into a chair next to Kat and gave her a pat on the shoulder, supportive and protective of the expectant mother. As they all were.

"Kat had a dream." Sami spit out the short explanation and sat down, hoping to hear what had her aunt unsettled. Kat had her own abilities, a water witch whose gift of perception had been heightened by recent contact with a Fae. A *good* Iele named Rook.

Tate took up a position by the fireplace. Quietly, she waited.

With all eyes on her, Kat rubbed her belly and drew a deep breath. "The dream was about vampires. They were chasing me down an alley." She shuddered. "I could barely run, because my stomach was so big. In the dream, anyway."

"Sweetheart." Brit kneeled beside her and took her fingers in his.

"I'm fine." She waved a dismissive hand. "Like I said, it was just so vivid and real. I definitely dream in color." She closed her eyes and shook all over again.

Blood. Sami curled her fingers into her thighs beneath the table. The color of red splashed behind her eyes again, as it had likely saturated Kat's nightmare.

She pushed aside her own unease and said, "Don't worry. We're staying on top of everything." She assured Kat with a firm tone and a big smile. "In fact, things have gotten so boring around here, magickally speaking, that I just spent an hour reading spells. For fun," she added with a twist of her lips.

"You?" Kat teased her with a light laugh. "I thought you already knew everything."

"Ha ha. I'm afraid you must be thinking of Tate."

"Hey," Tate protested, but like Sami, she fell right into the banter in an effort to distract Kat from what must have been a horrible dream. A woman running from blood-sucking fiends, trying to save the life of her unborn child.

Sami almost shuddered herself but pulled it together and joined her mother at the counter to help dole out the chicken pasta. In unspoken agreement, the family fell into conversation, carefully sidestepping any mention of the off-limit topics.

Even the word magick went utterly unwhispered.

As they ate, Fiona spoke excitedly about Ronan's return home, the soldier who'd begun as her enemy and ended as the man she loved. Kat leaned against Brit, and he kissed her temple, while Tate and Jack shared a grin.

Everyone seemed content and happy, eagerly looking to the future.

And that's exactly how Sami intended things to stay.

Sami brought the ring into their world, so she would be the one to keep it safe. To keep it secret. For the rest of her days, if that's what it took.

With her plate empty, she took a swig of tea and sent an innocent look to her mother. "May I have a brownie now?"

Her mother's mouth kicked up on one side with a cheeky smile. "Why don't you bring them to the table?"

"So the rest of us can have some before Sami eats them all," Brit said, holding out his plate to Sami.

She took it with a dramatic sigh. "At your service. Apparently." Smiling to herself, she moved to the counter and set down the dish.

Movement flashed past the window. Sami froze.

Now her instincts didn't tingle. They screamed. Her flesh chilled and her blood warmed—burning with the fire of magick. Flames of power rolled through her, sensing the danger.

    She peered into the night and said, "Something's here."

# 3

Sami glanced to Tate and Fiona before slipping out the door. Without having to be told, her sisters moved quietly and joined her in the light of a full summer moon. A soft *snick* came from behind them, their mother locking the door.

They'd come up with a plan in the event their home or property was ever invaded. Right now, their mother, grandfather, and Kat were all moving to an interior room while Brit and Jack exited the house on the far side from where Sami and her sisters now stood.

That way if things got ugly, they'd have a second line of defense taking the enemy by surprise.

Leaves rustled in the wind. Waves crashed on the cliffs. Despite the normal sounds, Sami cocked her head. She listened.

With a slight jerk of her chin, she indicated the front yard. She intentionally avoided stepping on the pavers, instead treading gently on the grass.

However softly she moved, the creature hiding in the shadows would know she was there. Night vision, acute sense of smell, blinding speed, and brutal strength. The beast stalking the night possessed them all.

Sami was the one who needed silence. So she could hear the attack coming.

In the front yard, she and her sisters spread out, each scanning the surrounding darkness. Watching. Waiting.

Sensing.

"It's out there," Tate said, curling her hands into fists, holding the white flames of her magick until the time was right.

"I know." Unlike her sister, Sami kept her arms and hands lax, opening herself up to hear the slightest noise. The presence of a threat seemed almost palpable, the air thicker and heavier, more oppressive.

A crunching noise echoed from the tree line straight ahead, and she zeroed in on the spot beneath a huge maple. As she stared, the darkness shifted. A tall male figure glided from the shadows.

"So finally the witches have come out to play." Black as pitch, his eyes darted between the three women, and a cocky half-smile lifted one side of his mouth.

To bare a single fang.

Sami stayed calm but channeled the heat of her power. She and her sisters had dealt with the Fae beings, but this was their first time going up against this breed of Iele. The creature before them possessed inhuman speed and might, not to mention the fangs. Long, sharp, and deadly.

"You know why I'm here," he said, his voice dropping to a snarl. "I won't return empty-handed." He crouched, prepared to leap.

But Sami was ready. "You made a big mistake coming here." She lifted her hands, ghostly flames dancing in her palms. "And now you won't return at all."

He growled again, a deep, wet sound that reminded her again of Emuirdane's death. The fiend might have the lean beauty of the Fae, but now his face twisted in fury, revealing his true nature. His thirst for blood.

The Iele sprang, his unnatural strength thrusting him up and toward Sami. But Sami and Tate released their power, striking him mid-leap with scorching fire.

Howling, the Iele dropped to the ground. Wrath and the lust for her blood burned red in his eyes. He tried to move, but he remained on the ground, burning, as Fiona held him down with her magick.

Sami pulled a dagger from the hilt at her waist. Sharp steel fused with gold, the only metal poisonous to Iele. "Did you really think you could take us?" She huffed out a short laugh and approached the fiend writhing on the lawn.

His eyes—still the color of murder—dilated with fear. Yet he challenged her. "You can't beat us all. When my King comes, you all will die. You will be drained into lifeless shells."

She kneeled beside him, certain of Fee's ability to keep him pinned. "That may be," she raised the dagger, "but not tonight." She plunged the blade into his chest.

Steel pierced his heart and gold entered his system. When the poison hit, he convulsed, shaking all over as he died.

Standing, Sami watched his body shrivel to a gray husk.

Tate and Fiona moved to flank her. "We've already started a fire," Tate said. "Might as well finish him off."

"We don't know if that will even work." Fiona folded her arms across her stomach, a squeamish expression on her face. Ever kindhearted, she disliked killing anything. Even a Fae monster who'd come to make her his meal.

"We might as well learn now. If we can burn them completely, we may not even need gold." Tate called forth her fire again but held it at bay, the ivory light blending with that of the full moon.

Sami and Fiona did the same, and as one, they directed their palms toward the dead Iele.

"Stop!" Another male emerged from the shadows but halted abruptly when Sami turned her fire in his direction.

He stood frozen, one palm up in a halting gesture.

Sami looked him over. Hair and eyes dark as midnight. Tough muscles and hard lines conveyed brute strength. He wore all black, to blend with the dark, but like his cohort, he'd made a mistake coming into the light.

Sami sauntered closer, grinning. "Well, you're a handsome one, aren't you?" Her smile morphed into a glare. "Too bad you're a leech." She fired at the new intruder.

And missed.

~~~

White heat shot toward Grayson. He threw himself to the ground, rolled, and regained his feet in a move he'd performed hundreds of times. Only never to escape a fire-throwing female hellbent on his death.

He held up his hands. "Wait a —"

She blasted him again, and this time he barely escaped, the stream of flames singeing his pants.

"You're fast," she said. "Too fast for a human."

Grayson slapped a hand at his charred pants. He was beginning to take this personally. Following the trail here tonight, he'd expected to find the ones he hunted, eliminate them, and make them disappear before anyone else encountered them or got hurt.

That plan was well and truly blown. Not only were there three witnesses, but he'd arrived in time to see the women kill a vampire. Not the turned humans he usually dealt with, but originals. *Iele.*

He had more questions now than after leaving the warehouse in Bangor, but first, he had to talk sense into the enraged woman. "I *am* human." He fell into a fighting stance, relying on a lifetime of training to defend himself. "Not sure I can say the same for you."

His comment caught her off guard, uncertainty flashing across her features before she made her decision and narrowed her eyes. He recognized the determined look of someone reloading a weapon.

"Just wait, damn it."

The woman shook her head, giving movement to her long, loose curls. "People don't move like you. And why would you be out here with a bloodsucker unless you were one, too?"

Still ready to evade, Grayson kept his gaze locked on her. "Because I tracked them here."

"Tracked?" she asked, holding off her attack for another blessed moment.

A woman with black hair short as a boy's stepped forward. "Them?" she asked in a soft voice, definitely less hostile than the other. "As in more than one?"

"Yes." Grayson risked turning his attention to her. "And he's still here." *I can smell him.* But he'd save the explanations for later. First priority—eliminate the threat.

After he convinced these three not to roast him alive as they'd just done to the Iele on the ground. "We can talk after. I promise you, I'm not your enemy."

The tall woman who couldn't seem to rein in her fire only snorted. "We've heard that before."

Grayson would have offered more assurances, but the scent of raw meat washed over him, the overpowering stench announcing the presence of a vampire. But the vile smell was stronger than any he'd ever encountered, reaching down through his throat to grip his guts.

Instinctively, he reached back for his dirk, a blade crafted for hand-to-hand combat, modernized and coated in gold. Made to kill creatures of the night. He gripped the hilt and spun.

As the second vamp dropped from a tree.

Grayson positioned himself between the fiend and the women. Despite what he'd seen them do, he'd devoted his life to protecting people from what lurked in the shadows. And he'd die before breaking his sworn oath.

But the vamp ignored the others, his interest only for Grayson. He advanced with caution, head tilted as if bemused. Sniffing the air, he leaned forward. "What *are* you?"

Grayson paused but remained vigilant, his eyes tracking over the tall, muscled form. He was bigger than any vampire Grayson had ever seen, and there was something about the shape of his head, the sheen of his skin . . .

"You really are one of them." He gave voice to a truth that just wouldn't go away. "An *Iele*." His tongue almost tripped over the word. He'd seen the evidence in the warehouse, what had been done to that boy. He could see and scent the difference in the creature before him.

But his mind kept throwing up barriers, trying to deny.

"You're not like other humans," the creature said, leering at Grayson. Then he slid a hateful look to the women. "Or the witches."

The Iele dragged his eyes back to Grayson. "I might keep you," he said, as if the idea had just struck. "I'll take you as a prize, and my king will reward me."

Filing away questions about witches and kings for a later time, Grayson released a breath and readied himself. The guy might be huge, might be an original Iele, but by his own admission, he didn't know what Grayson was.

Too bad for the smug bloodsucker. Because he was about to find out.

The vamp closed in, and Grayson stood his ground. He waited. He let him come.

When the Iele slipped into striking distance, Grayson lunged forward, slicing up and under the vamp's arm. He cut the artery inside the elbow, allowing specially crafted gold particles to transfer from his blade to the bastard's black blood.

The Iele hissed and clutched his arm.

But he didn't go down.

Another swift lunge and a more direct stab, just below the clavicle.

The vampire roared.

"So it's going to be a brawl," Grayson said, a secret thrill shooting through his veins. He shouldn't take pleasure in the challenge, but he hadn't faced a worthy adversary in years.

He lifted his dirk and motioned the beast forward with a crook of his hand. "Let's go then."

"I'll drink off of you slowly and still take you back to my king. The pain you'll endure will be legendary. And my glory will be—"

The vamp erupted in a white blaze, his surprised screams carrying up to the night sky.

The ill-tempered woman stepped forward and snuffed her flames with a clap of hands. "Enough." She stalked over to Grayson and gave him a once-over. "Tell me why I shouldn't kill you."

But he too had had enough. He shifted the tip of his blade toward her throat. "You could try."

"Both of you stop." The third woman rushed forward with a scolding expression. She pushed at her shoulder-length hair and blew out a breath to shake the stars. "Sami, he's obviously not one of them, and we don't go around attacking innocent people."

The one called Sami eyed him. "He's not innocent."

Her words caused a twinge in the center of his chest, and he wondered if the woman with the unruly hair was also psychic.

*Unruly.* Now why did that word seem to suit her so well?

He scowled, not only in response to her on-target comment, but also to bring himself back to center. He had no time to waste arguing while two original specimens lay smoldering on the grass.

He turned away from Sami to address the more rational female, but two men walked up, suspicion hardening their features. "What's going on, Tate?" Light-haired and holding a gleaming axe, one of them stalked to the woman's side.

A man with darker coloring and an ancient-looking crossbow held back, his stare lasered on Grayson as he spoke. "We watched you take out the other two," he said to the women in general, "so who is this?"

Five witnesses. Magickal abilities. Not-your-every-day weaponry. Grayson had no idea what he'd walked into, but he had to get the situation under control.

Calling forth a calm but authoritative voice, he said, "I don't know who all of you are or how you're involved in this, but I need you to step back and let me do what I came to do."

The soft-spoken female with short hair eased closer. "What did you come to do?"

"Oh, fuck that." Angry curls was back again. Sami. That was her name.

"Here's what's going to happen," she said, stepping into Grayson's line of sight so all he saw was her. Her eyes were dark, liquid pools. And they roiled with fury. "We're torching these bloodsuckers, and then you're coming inside to explain yourself. I don't care what you came here to do, but this," she pointed to the vamp at his feet, "is none of your business."

"That's where you're wrong." His stare never wavered from hers as he pulled out his cell phone. "This is exactly my business." He punched a single number to contact his team. Dodge answered.

Breaking eye contact at last, he turned his back on her and quietly gave instructions. When he finished, he addressed the group. "You can try to stop me, but that would be a waste of all of our time and energy. I will answer your questions soon, and believe me, I have some of my own. But first, I'm going to take care of these bodies."

"No. This is our home. This is our town." Sami reached out and gripped his upper arm. "We have the situation under control."

"Obviously, you don't, or I wouldn't be here." Allowing some of his own anger to surface, he pulled free and flung his hand toward the grass. "Those are two original Iele. In *our* world." He swept a scathing glance over the gathering. "You all seem far too familiar with their kind, so tell me," he focused on Sami, "why the hell are *they* here?"

# 4

Castle Sangridor
The Ielonaar Realm

Malrik waited as the guard unlocked the door from the other side. Groaning low, the metal slab swung in on its hinges, opening to what appeared to be eternal darkness.

"A moment, Your Majesty." Vale, Malrik's consul and advisor, walked inside ahead of him and spoke in hushed tones with the guard.

Stepping through the doorway, Malrik peered down into a great black square. Then the guard lit a torch from a sconce, the bright burst of flame illuminating a staircase. Carved in stone, the steps ran along the perimeter, descending into a depth of shadows.

Malrik motioned for the guard to take the lead. The fire from his torch cast golden light and gave glimpses of what resided in the walls. Alcoves filled with bones, skeletons replete with swords and shields, the remains of ancient warriors forever interred.

He housed only certain prisoners here—in the dark, and among the dead—family members of the mages and magickans he'd taken hostage. They lived daily under the threat of torture and pain, should their gifted relatives refuse to cooperate.

The magick workers themselves lived elsewhere, treated more kindly and in far better living quarters. Guilt and fear, Malrik knew, often served as the strongest of chains.

In silence, the three of them continued downward. As they neared the deeper levels, dankness rose up from below, moldy and stale, the only sound a distant trickle of water.

After a time, they reached the bottom, where a ribbon of dark liquid flowed. Four corridors led to different segments of the tombs, but Malrik entered the one directly ahead.

Here at the lowest level, the interconnected rooms had been made into cells, fashioned with manacles and bars. Malrik stopped at a wooden panel set into the stone wall. The guard moved quickly, hastening to unlock the door.

Inside, light abounded, emanating from scattered candles, fire set beneath a cauldron, and whatever foul concoction brewed within the black vessel. The room contained shelves lined with bottles, books, and dried herbs. A witch's lair.

"Your Majesty." A young woman in ragged clothing clambered from a thin blanket on the floor. The pathetic scrap served as her bed, the bowl of mush beside it her dinner. She gave an awkward curtsy, and when she stood again, she kept her head bowed.

"You have information?" Malrik asked. The only reason he'd come down to the gloomy bowels of this place had been for news of the scouts he'd sent to the human world. Though not one of the magick workers he'd taken prisoner, the woman claimed to be a soothsayer. She'd sworn to be of value.

Her life depended on it.

"I've l-l-lost sight of your scouts," she stuttered, the fear of delivering bad news shaking her voice. Gaze still averted, she began wringing her hands. "I felt them strongly until an hour ago."

"And?"

She hazarded a quick glance at him before moving to her cauldron. She floated her hand over the deep purple ooze. Jerking back suddenly, she shook her head. "The connection has snapped. I've tried everything to get them back, but I fear . . ." She gulped and finished in a whisper. "I fear they are dead."

Malrik cast her a look of disdain. "You are certain?"

"I'm not certain. But I feel strongly—"

"Quiet." Though not shouted, his order echoed in the chamber. "Your father failed to serve me, and you remember what happened to him."

The woman quivered, eyes round as perfect brown pebbles. She did not speak.

"Upon his death, I allowed you to live." He lifted a finger. "I allowed you this chamber and the tools of your craft, on the promise you would provide me with sight, with awareness of what transpired in the human world."

"And I can. If only—"

"Silence," Malrik said.

"Your Majesty, please let me—"

"Silence!" His voice boomed like a cannon in the small space. "I gain nothing from vague *feelings*, which is all you have offered. You've wasted enough of my time." Having his final say, he turned his back on her. A death sentence.

"Please," she cried, throwing herself to the floor to grasp at his ankles. Tears left trails on her dirty face. "I can do better."

With a snort of distaste, Malrik lifted one leg and drove his heel into her chest. She collapsed into a ball and wailed.

Ignoring the sobs behind him, he spoke to the guard. "I'm done with this one."

"To the leeching chamber, Sire?"

A response in the affirmative rose to Malrik's tongue, but then he thought better of it. He insisted on making an example of any who failed him, but especially those who made false promises.

"No," he said, pausing beside the burly man. "She is yours. Drain her if you like or share her with your men."

The guard's expression changed to one of glee mixed with something else. Something . . . *vicious*. "Thank you, Your Majesty." His lecherous gaze tracked to the woman on the floor. "She is young and strong."

Malrik understood his leer. Despite her torn and filthy clothing, the woman was comely. He inclined his head. "She is yours to do with as you wish."

Exiting into the corridor with Vale, Malrik released an angry curse and drove a fist into his palm. "I've stalled long enough, a waste of time. I must find that ring."

Damn those interfering witches. If the Whiteburn sisters were ever foolish enough to cross his path again, he'd drain them of their blood, and their magick. He'd suck them down to the sweet of their marrow.

"Everything I've planned hinges on that ring." Malrik fumed. "I must have it."

Halting, he gripped Vale's arm. "What I need is a true oracle." He stared past his consul and into the shadows. "A blind seer." One with the gift of vision, enhanced by the loss of actual eyesight.

A wicked smile curved Malrik's mouth. "And I know where to find one."

"Sire?" Vale instilled the question with weight, tilting his head. "You gave your word."

"This is war. Unpleasantries can no longer be avoided." Malrik pressed his tongue against his fang, frustration throbbing through him, all the way into the sharp point.

He would visit the leeching chamber himself and slake his thirst in the ways of old.

As he imagined the warm, coppery tang rolling down his throat, a scream pierced the air, so shrill that Malrik and Vale both turned back.

The guard was dragging the young witch from her cell, aided by two other hulking sentries. One of them slapped the woman, splitting her lip before reaching down to rip her blouse.

The sight of her pale breasts drew a cheer from the third man, who then picked up her legs to help carry her down the hall. Her pleas and screams ricocheted in the narrow corridor, but the men hauled her deeper into the tombs, to the temporary living quarters.

Filled with at least twenty guards.

With no concern for the woman's fate, Malrik faced Vale. "I want that seer. I *will* have her." He stomped toward the stairs, forcing Vale to grab a torch from the wall and race to catch up. "Ready the troops."

"And what of the ring?" Vale asked, hurrying to light the way for his king. "Shall I send more scouts?"

"No," Malrik said, starting back up the stairs, passing the bones of Iele who'd come before him. "Scouts are clearly no match for the witches." Three human sisters defeating his men? Such disgrace could not be borne.

"I'll not tolerate another defeat, so henceforth, we do what we must. We will peel the skin from every human. We will drink their children before their eyes. Whatever needs be done, the Daughters of Nadia *will* return my ring."

Malrik lowered his voice, the hushed tone crawling in the darkness like insects over flesh. "No more hiding. No more scouts. Now, we fill their streets with blood."

·In the low light of flame, he turned to Vale. "Send the hunters."

# 5

Holding information for ransom had been the perfect way to get the infuriating Grayson exactly where Sami wanted him—on her turf, in the light of day, and surrounded by her family.

After he'd taken the two dead Iele and made his show of authority, Sami had realized the kind of man they were dealing with. So she'd stonewalled him.

Then he'd stonewalled her.

Her stubborn refusal to answer his questions about the Iele presence—and Fiona's gentle persuasion—had convinced him to return to the Whiteburn house the following morning. Without his men.

This was a condition Sami had insisted on. "I won't have a gang of hulking strangers scaring my mother. She's fragile," she'd told him, biting the inside of her cheek to suppress a smile. Her mother had survived more than most people could imagine.

But the ploy had worked, and here he was, striding up the path to the front door as if he owned the place. Peeking through the beveled glass of the front door, Sami narrowed her eyes. "Look at him swagger," she muttered under her breath.

"Will you just go?" Fiona swatted her lightly on the arm. "Hostility won't help anyone. We need him to talk to us, Sami. He and whoever else he works with might be allies, and at the very least, he has information."

Sami grunted.

Fiona latched on to her ear and pulled like an eighteenth-century school marm. "Go."

"Ow!" Sami wiggled free. "Okay, okay. I'm gone." Rubbing her ear, she followed the main hallway to the rear of the house, joining Tate, Jack, Brit, and her grandfather in the back parlor. Noticing Kat's absence, Sami assumed she was still sleeping or, more likely, plagued by morning sickness.

Elegant yet comfortable, the spacious room offered plenty of seating and a view of the back lawn through a spread of French patio doors. A thick stand of trees rimmed the grass, allowing only glimpses of the deep blue Atlantic beyond.

"He's here," Sami stated simply, taking up a position near the doors, the morning sun warm on her back but doing little to improve her disposition. She felt the annoying need to be standing when Grayson entered. Fiona might think he could be an ally, but to Sami, the man was everything adversary.

Fiona's welcoming voice carried lightly from the front, followed by a low rumble that had to be Grayson.

"Relax," Brit said as he came to her side.

"What?" Sami all but snapped.

"You're tense as a board."

Sami scowled. Was it that obvious? Instantly, she let her arms fall and rolled her neck.

"He's only one man. There are seven of us." Using the mug of coffee he held, Brit gestured to encompass the room. "And based on how he reacted last night, I don't think he can fend off magick."

On that Sami agreed, but she wasn't convinced that Grayson was *just* a man. The second Iele had been too curious about him, almost . . . in awe. Who was Grayson, and what made him so compelling?

More questions swirled to the surface of her mind but were shoved back down when he entered the parlor. He trailed behind Fiona, drawing Sami's full attention.

He'd paired jeans with a shirt as black as his hair, yet his bearing somehow made the casual clothing seem like a uniform. He quickly assessed the room and its occupants, lingering on Sami a second too long.

Fiona held out her hand. "Please, sit and make yourself comfortable," she said, drawing the slightest nod from their guest.

Sami still didn't like him, and she definitely didn't trust him. He just had an edge about him, like a soldier, but something else that whispered of mercenary. Or assassin. The kind of man who worked best hidden in shadow.

But he had information to give, and she wanted it all.

He took the offered seat and Fiona made introductions. "You remember Tate and Sami from last night. Brit and Jack." She gestured to each of them. "And this is our grandfather."

Sami studied her grandfather as he studied Grayson. The older man's eyes scrutinized beneath a wrinkled brow, but he stayed silent.

When she shifted back to Grayson, she found his dark gaze locked on her. She'd never seen eyes such a deep brown, the piercing quality enhanced by straight brows.

As he stared, an itch began between her shoulder blades, an urge to move or reposition her body. If she didn't know any better, she'd say she felt self-conscious. But that didn't make any sense. She'd faced far greater threats.

But when he looked away, her breath expelled. One she hadn't realized she'd been holding.

Rebuilding her mental wall, Sami decided to take control and start the conversation—interrogation if she had her way—but her mother chose that moment to breeze into the room with a large tray in her hands. "I've got coffee and tea," she announced, so cheerfully it set Sami's teeth on edge.

A square table of sand-colored wood sat in the center of the sofas and chairs. Her mother approached to set down the tray with cups, carafes, and—was that a basket of strawberry scones?

Crossing her arms, Sami ground her jaws together and reminded herself that she and her mother had very different methodologies. Like Fiona, Nadia Whiteburn was all heart.

Sami was all hammer.

Grayson stood to intercept the heavy tray. "Let me help you with that," he said, his hard mouth transforming into a radiant smile and eyes crinkling in a way that was far too charming.

"Oh, thank you." Sami's mother beamed. "Coffee or tea?" she asked, plating a scone before he could accept or deny.

"Coffee, black. Thank you."

This time, a sound of disgust burst from Sami's lips.

Her mother sent a sharp, reprimanding glance over her shoulder and picked up a carafe, continuing on as if this were a Sunday tea party.

Sami caught Tate's eye, glowered, then jerked her chin in Grayson's direction. Sami couldn't trust her tongue at the moment but knew Tate could carry off the role of diplomat—the deft hand between heart and hammer.

"Grayson," Tate began, "I'm sure you're as ready as we are to get this started." She also took a cup and poured herself some coffee, maintaining the gracious pretense while getting down to business. Then she looked directly at Sami. "Why don't we all sit?"

Swallowing a grumble, Sami moved to the pale blue couch opposite the table from Grayson while Tate slid into the matching chair beside his. Everyone else sat as well, instantly reducing the tense mood.

Even Sami schooled her features into a serene expression. She'd given Tate the lead and would play the supportive second. They'd make no progress if everyone remained on guard.

But damned if she was going to butter his scone.

"I appreciate your having me into your home," Grayson addressed them all, "especially considering the circumstances."

Sami leaned back against soft powder-blue fabric. *Oh, he's a smooth one.* So very polite and civilized, almost nothing like the bull-headed man who'd eagerly challenged a monster to a fight.

"We got off on the wrong foot last night," he continued, "but I believe we have more in common than not. The Iele called the three of you witches, and I saw for myself what you can do with your extraordinary abilities." He sipped his coffee and set it down. "So I'm guessing you understand the importance of safeguarding sensitive information."

Now he homed in on Sami. "And that what I share with you today must be treated with discretion."

"Fine," she replied, since he'd felt the need to single her out. "You don't tell on us, and we don't tell on you."

"We have no reason to betray your confidence," Fiona added, softening Sami's blunt delivery with her placid tone. "We've seen a lot in our dealings with the Iele, but you're the first person outside of our family to know anything about them."

"And it's best to keep it that way, for the safety of others." Grayson propped his forearms on his knees and leaned forward companionably. "I live by a strict code, and I had no choice but to get involved. But truth be told, you caught me off guard." He angled his head and gave a half-smile. "First time I've seen anyone shoot flames from their hands."

This drew grins from the other women, but Sami's calm expression could have been made of steel.

"You should know that my objective, first and always, is the protection of civilians. And the containment of Iele." Now his easy smile disappeared. "The one from last night mentioned a king."

Chills ran down Sami's neck and out over her shoulders.

"Do you know who he meant?" Grayson focused on Fiona, likely thinking her a soft target. "Or where he's located?"

Despite her natural compassion, Fiona was no fool. She looked at Sami, who then looked at Tate.

Tate took a moment to consider her answer. "Not here. He lives in another realm but is able to send a small number of his people here." Short, to the point, and scarce on details.

Sami might have sent her sister a sly grin if not for the disquiet brought on by the mention of the king. King Malrik. The war-mongering Iele who possessed Emuirdane's brooch, the accompanying piece to the ring Sami had taken. Their green jewels contained the wealth of Emuirdane's magick.

And Malrik coveted them both.

Sami stared down at the floral rug, ashamed of her contributions to the family saga. Tate had outwitted the Winter Queen of Faerie, getting Sami, Fiona, and Jack all safely home. Then Fiona had followed up by freeing the Jeweled Ceffyl and rescuing an innocent baby from death.

And what had Sami done? She'd foolishly stolen the enchanted ring, drawing Malrik's blood-filled gaze to her world, and to her loved ones.

"You say your goal is to contain the Iele." Sami's grandfather spoke suddenly, gripping the silvered-handled cane he was never without but didn't use. Not until he needed the long, thin sword hidden within. "Just how many others have been in our world?"

Grayson hesitated, as if spilling details on this topic went against his grain. "Enough to be a problem, to be a threat. But they aren't like the ones from last night."

"You called the ones we killed originals." Sami's statement drew that penetrating gaze of his. "What did you mean?"

Grayson paused, his expression intense, as if he searched for the right way to explain. "The ones we track are essentially left over from the last time true Iele came to this world. We don't know how or why they came here, but after they'd gone or been destroyed, they left behind a type of offspring."

"And these offspring are also killed by gold." Jack made a gesture as if holding a knife. "The dagger you used had a gold component, didn't it?"

"Yes." Grayson seemed to be reevaluating Jack. The man whose weapon of choice was an axe. "Our version of a wooden stake. You've probably seen movies or read books about vampires, how they bite a victim and transform them into something else."

"Vampires." Sami's mother set down her cup with a *clink*. "We already knew some Iele drank blood, but that word conjures so many disturbing images."

Grayson stilled. "*Some* of them? How many have you come into contact with?"

At that, Sami and the others simply glanced at each other. Where to begin? Emuirdane? Hellana? The farworld of Faerie?

"We'll get to that," she said. It wasn't time to divulge the whole story. Sitting forward, she mirrored his earlier body language. But when she rested her arms on her legs, she steepled her fingers together and frowned.

"I want to know how you and two other men just *happened* to be nearby with a black van, ready and waiting to haul off those bodies. How did you know where to find them?"

When he only stared at her, Sami said, "These weren't the first Iele we've seen in Bar Harbor, but it's the first we've seen of you. So why are you here? Why now?"

Grayson didn't speak, he didn't move, other than a barely perceptible tightening around the eyes. The entire room held a collective breath.

At last, he said, "Because this is where the body was found."

Sami jolted, as if a huge wasp had stung the center of her chest. She went rigid, her muscles constricting. "What body?"

Tate and Brit both burst out with questions while Fiona put a hand to her stomach. Sami was aware of the others' reactions around her, but she couldn't concentrate with the buzzing in her head and the blurring of her eyes.

She'd sensed a foreign presence nearby, a malevolence that had grown stronger over the last several days. She'd known something was coming. She'd *known*.

Now the intuition she'd ignored had fallen deathly silent. Smothered by guilt.

*This is my fault. I brought them here.* Recriminations battered her, blow after blow, heavy knocks weighed down with self-blame. Why hadn't she cast a foresight spell? Or asked Kat to try one of her new water tricks? Maybe if Sami had seen, if she'd understood what was really going on, she could have stopped the Iele before anyone else had been hurt.

Before anyone had been killed.

"Who was it?" Her voice creaked out in a ragged whisper. Slowly, she stood, the action gaining Grayson's notice. She impaled him with her eyes. "Who was it?"

"He hasn't been identified yet, but we've got people working on that." His tone was firm but mild, as he'd obviously picked up on Sami's distress.

"You've got people?" A harsh sound erupted from her throat. "How many people? Are you part of some underground organization? Or one funded by our own government?"

Grayson shook his head, but she ignored him and continued her rant. It felt good to spew out the disgust and resentment. Disgust for herself. Resentment for him. Why the hell did this stranger know that someone in her hometown had been killed by a Fae, but she didn't?

And she had caused it by bringing that damned ring back with her. Hell, she'd all but clanged the dinner bell, ensuring innocent people would be served up on platters.

No. She shook her hand and her head in hot denial. No one else would die.

She edged around the table, closer to Grayson. "Tell me who you are and what you're a part of. Last night, you said you'd tracked the Iele here. How exactly did you do that?"

"Sami, calm down."

Tate's words rolled right over her.

"No more evading. If people are dying, you have to tell us everything." Sami couldn't stop herself, too agitated, too churned up by a potent mix of suspicion and shame.

And Grayson had delivered both.

"You're not really what you say you are." She'd sensed it from the moment he'd strolled out of the darkness. "You move too fast, and the Iele was way too interested in you, especially considering what he came for."

Grayson stilled. "What did he come for?"

"No more trading." As if she hadn't heard his question, she made a slicing motion through the air. "You're not leaving this house until you tell me."

"Sami!"

Her mother's outraged cry barely penetrated Sami's fury.

"Tell me who you are," she demanded, palms heating. Her fire ached for release. "Better yet, tell me *what* you are."

# 6

Grayson considered it a triumph of will that he remained seated. The urge to meet Sami Whiteburn head-to-head did a slow burn through his veins before exploding in his brain.

But he couldn't afford to react. He had to keep his mind on the mission—stay centered, stay focused. So he'd do that, and still fight her fire. With a shield of ice.

Calling on years of making snap judgments in tricky situations, he dropped a cold shutter over his personal feelings and forced himself to go through the motions. Autopilot was nothing new. But instead of throwing a roundhouse to an opponent's head, he reached for the plate holding his scone.

And tried not to break it with his clenched fingers.

Absently, he sniffed the pastry, meeting her tirade with pure yet painful patience. "You're right. I'm more than human."

Sami stepped back, his easy admission stunning her into silence.

Albeit, a temporary one.

"Then what?" She gave him a scathing onceover as if searching for clues. "You move so quickly, almost like—"

"A bloodsucker?" He tossed out the word and beat her to the punch. "I assure you—again—that I am not." The smile he sent her was razor-sharp. "I accepted your invitation and came here for a reason, so I will tell you my history. What I know of it, at least."

Tate sat up straighter in her chair. "Sami," she said, instilling subtle warning in her sister's name.

"Sit down." Sami's mother, however, was not subtle at all.

Grayson suppressed a smile and slid a glance to the Whiteburn matriarch. *Fragile, my ass.* But he had to give Sami points for her little maneuver.

And since she appeared to be relenting, Grayson waited, delaying any further explanation until Sami tossed her hands up and went back to the sofa. Still, she refused to take her eyes off of him.

At least some color had returned to her face, and despite her combative attitude, he was glad to see it. A flush of fury was better than pallor, more assuring than her drain to white after learning about the Iele murder victim. She'd taken the news hard, her reaction much more pronounced than the rest of her family.

The question was why?

Last night she'd been defensive, obstinate, and wary. Now her anger seemed almost desperate, and Grayson couldn't help wondering what fueled her sudden wrath.

He'd need all the pieces before he was done and would draw them out in due time. But for now he'd make a lateral move, his first in this game of give-and-pull. Assuming the volatile Sami continued to play nice.

Diverting his stare from the stubborn woman, he distributed his focus between the others and began. "I belong to an organization that has been in existence longer than anyone can accurately pinpoint. We have no official name and refer to ourselves in generic terms—the organization, the company, the firm. Staying unremarkable and unnoticeable is imperative. Society is better off not knowing what we do or, especially, what we protect them from."

When no one challenged him on this, he went on. "As far as what gives some of us special attributes, the only definitive thing I can tell you is that it's hereditary."

"You have relatives who are like you?" Brit asked. His resemblance to the women was clear, all sharing the same dark hair. Except for Sami, of course, with her fiery undertones.

"Actually, both of my parents had talents. You might say it's a family business."

Brit barked a short laugh. "I can relate to that."

Grayson acknowledged the commonality with a tip of his head. "The legacy comes with responsibility, an intrinsic part of our heritage. Originally, we started with ten families, clans with a common goal, a common enemy. Over the years, new blood has been slowly introduced."

"So what exactly *are* your abilities?" This from Fiona, who didn't seem confrontational at all, merely curious.

Grayson cleared his throat before listing a few of his traits. "Enhanced eyesight and sense of smell." He glanced to Sami. "Faster-than-normal reflexes." His fingers tightened again on the dainty plate. The higher-ups had already cleared this meeting—deciding potential gain to be worth the risk—but telling these things to strangers still made him uncomfortable.

"As far as how we came to be this way, the debate has gone on for years. Some believe we have Iele blood, not from being bitten and changed, but from the mating of an Iele and a human."

"Is that possible?" Tate wrinkled her nose.

"Sounds distasteful to me, too," he told her. "Which is why I prefer the second theory, that we co-evolved with the beasts we hunt, like in nature, predator and prey. And *they* are the prey."

He let his statement hang in the air before continuing. "Yet some hold another belief. They think we've been blessed by the gods, chosen to defend our home and our people."

Fiona's big green eyes shone with sincerity. "You seem skeptical, but the blessing of a deity is very possible." When Grayson smiled indulgently, a wrinkle formed between her brows and her tone grew more serious. "My sisters and I have visited the home of a goddess. She is called the Dea Matrona and has entire armies serving her will to defend the innocent."

Drawing a slow breath, he gathered his thoughts and tried to process her incredible claim. He did his best to hide his uncertainty. He didn't want to offend anyone else, since Sami was already pissed off enough for the whole group.

"You've been to the home of a goddess?" he asked at last. "How? And where?"

Fiona bit her lower lip as if realizing she'd revealed too much.

Carefully, Grayson set down the plate. "You're serious." He waited for more, but when no one spoke, he lifted a shoulder and began backtracking. If he pushed too hard, he might lose the tenuous bit of trust he'd gained. "I guess anything is possible, and given what I do for a living, nothing should surprise me."

He tossed an *aw-shucks* grin to Fiona.

In response, she stopped biting her lip. "Yes. Just as we shouldn't be surprised there are others who know about the Fae."

As silence stretched, it became clear she would offer nothing more, so Grayson did instead. "It's just that we have books dating back to the beginning, and there's no mention of deities. Not even a hint. Only details on the enemy and the best ways to kill them."

"And that's what brought you to our home. The intent to kill Iele." Sami commented more calmly this time, her temper having subsided the slightest bit. "Is that how you tracked them to our house? This special sight you have? Your sense of smell?"

"Both," Grayson said casually. "Iele, and their offspring, leave evidence of where they've been. Not only can I see, hear, and smell what others can't, but I've also had intensive training since childhood. I know what to look for."

"Since you were a child?" Sami's hard edge softened even further, her posture relaxing. "Surely you didn't go out looking for vampires as a kid."

His lips thinned in automatic response, but he caught himself and forced a friendly expression back onto his face. "When I was ready." *Or thought I was ready.*

Memories he often struggled to keep at bay suddenly flashed in vivid color. He could picture that night as if it played before him on a screen. He could feel it, like a virtual reality. The sweet warmth of a Southern spring, a scrape of magnolia leaves in the breeze, the scent of yellow jasmine.

Then the foul odor of beasts, emerging from the shadows in numbers greater than they'd expected. He'd been primed for the fight, ready to prove himself. But it had been too soon, and he'd been too young. Too cocky.

Tension clamped the base of Grayson's skull. Recognizing the signs of stress, he blinked away the tainted past and inhaled strawberry scone, strong coffee, and the faint but pleasant citrus smell of the Whiteburn household.

Here and now was all that mattered. True Iele had breached the human world again, their presence a plague just waiting to spread. So there could be no errors, no missed opportunities. When the average person made a mistake, repercussions happened.

But when Grayson made a mistake, massacres happened.

Muscles stiff, resolve unbending, he renewed his focus on Sami. "The king mentioned last night, I need to know more about him and why he's sending his men here. You said they came for something. What is it?"

Her jaw dropped in surprise at having the tables turned on her, but she recovered quickly and snapped her mouth shut. "Fair enough," she said with a huff.

She rubbed her hands over her thighs and rested them on her knees. "His name is Malrik. He rules over the blood-drinking Iele."

"Are you saying there are others that don't drink blood?"

"Yes." She glanced away from him, to Tate, and then Fiona. "As far as we can tell."

"So why is sending his followers here now?" Grayson paused for a beat, and then homed in on the more crucial aspect. "And what do they want from you?"

Before leaving the night before, he'd noted various tracks circling the Whiteburn home. Some had been days old. The creatures had been here before.

Sami returned her gaze to him. "He thinks we can help him locate a relic." Using her fingers, she tucked a long, curly strand behind her ear and lowered her lashes. Twice.

The hairs on the back of Grayson's neck tingled. Why was she lying?

Shrugging, she gave him a smile. One of the fakest smiles he'd ever seen. *She's holding something back.*

Which meant it was the time for him to change tactics—and pull harder. "What kind of relic and why does he think—"

A woman with pale blonde hair and wild eyes burst into the room. "I was running a bath. Staring at the water." Her words bulleted out between hitched breaths as she tied the belt of a pink satin robe.

Brit jumped up and ran to her, concern etching hard lines in his face. "Kat, what's wrong? Are you okay?" He gripped her upper arms.

"I'm fine, but I . . . sensed something. My mind just went white and cloudy, and I felt him."

"Who?" Sami asked. Now both she and Tate leapt up.

Grayson sat perfectly still, paying attention to every word.

"Rook," Kat said, rubbing her throat. "It was the water. Our connection."

"Who's Rook?" Grayson asked softly.

Sami fired an irritated glance his way. "An Iele."

"But a good one," Fiona hurriedly added.

Keeping a neutral expression in place, Grayson only nodded. He'd just begun making headway here, so for now he'd keep his opinion to himself.

That the only good Iele was a dead one.

He didn't show any outward reaction, other than to grind his fingers into his knee. Exactly what kind of relationship did these people have with the Fae? And how many did they deem to be *good*?

"I didn't actually hear him or get a message," the newly-arrived Kat explained, holding on to Brit for support, "but I felt his emotions. He was upset, worried."

"About Malrik?" Tate asked.

"Is the family in danger?" Sami's grandfather stood with the agility of a much younger man. And he didn't use his cane.

"No, it's not about us or our world. I think it has to do with the Ielonaar Realm." Kat stared up at Brit with fearful eyes. "He was rushing, running, and he was scared."

Shaking her head, she exhaled sharply. "He was terrified."

# 7

Royal Palace of Vei Lani
The Ielonaar Realm


Rook's heart thrashed within his chest, the erratic *thud-thud-thud* boosted by a rush of fear. He'd been in the map room, studying the distant land of Gellyn, when he'd merely glanced down into his cup of tea. And the vision arose, clamped around him with prophecy's merciless hands.

Bloodshed. Mutilation. Rape. The destruction of an entire kingdom, and all of its people. For the pursuit of a single woman.

Still caught in the throes of the horrible sights he'd seen, Rook raced down the palace corridor, burst through a curtained doorway, and exited onto a wide terrace. Dodging thick pillars, he sped toward the sandstone steps and wound his way down to the hanging gardens.

An arched gateway opened to a path leading to the beach, to the white sands and perfect waters of the Vei Lanian shore.

Two women and several small children played in the gentle waves, their laughter full-throated and carefree. And why shouldn't it be? Vei Lani had always been a place of harmony, of joy and tranquility. And one of the few—the very few—left in peace by the rampaging King Malrik.

But the violence Rook had seen in his mind, the carnage and

slaughter, cast a menacing shadow over his sunny homeland.

Even the far reaches of Vei Lani were now in peril, and so many innocent Fae would die. Unless he stopped it.

Without a moment to spare, he ran across the hot sand, but turned away from the blue sea, following a trail to the jungle instead. Uphill he rushed, tearing through the lush greenery.

His magick relied on water, and while the ocean was vast and deep, Corrina's Pond was still and dark. He would need those sacred waters to travel, and his aim must be precise. For he knew exactly where to go.

Small birds chattered brightly, hopping to-and-fro in the wild redfern growing around the pond. When he dashed to the water's edge, they winged up to the sky in a panic.

Uttering a quick chant to summon the conduit, Rook leapt into the cool, black depths.

And erupted from the surface of an entirely different place.

Water streamed down his face as he took in his surroundings and large swimming pool in which he floated. Smooth, Fae-polished stone lined the basin, their mix of colors turning the liquid a pure, jade green.

A decadent courtyard spread before him—huge flowering plants in ornamental vases, thick bright pillows, and wood furniture polished to a rich sheen. A place of luxury, fit for royalty, yet softened by a female's touch.

Slowly, Rook emerged from the water, in search of the one he'd come to find. Dripping on the patterned stone tiles, he stopped to listen. A woman's voice carried from beyond a large bush covered with yellow blossoms. Her words whispered, her tone soothing.

In haste, he rounded the shrubbery, drawing a slight startle from the lady of the residence. The queen of the castle.

In one smooth motion she rose, with a babe held to her chest, and took up a fighting stance. Blue daggers shot from her eyes. "Who are you?"

Rook took in the picture she presented—maternal, seductive, and fierce all at once. Something inside of him clutched and released.

"Hellana," he said on a breath, giving voice to her name in place of his own. "I mean you no harm."

She turned a cheek toward him, her gaze hard and suspicious. The movement released a blue tendril of hair. It draped down one side of her heart-shaped face. "I asked you a question."

Mother, fighter, and now . . . the imperious ruler. Rook was equally fascinated by them all, but he had no time to waste on formalities.

"My name is Rook," he offered, hoping to push beyond her initial distrust. He touched the center of his drenched chest. "I'm Vei Lanian, like you."

She scoffed, arcing one sea-colored brow. "Your hair gave that away." She smiled shrewdly. "And I see you're a water-drift. You must have traveled to my pool. That's the only explanation for your . . . *appearance*, and how you made your way past my guard."

Rook almost touched his hair, navy-blue and still sopping from his journey. He firmed his mouth instead and spoke sternly. "I've come to warn you. You're in danger." He hazarded a step closer, sure she would call for soldiers any minute. "You must come with me."

He'd expected her to laugh at first, or to rebuff him entirely, until he could persuade her. But her gaze grew sharp and calculating.

He reminded himself of her past troubles, and deceased husband. Emuirdane had been a cruel fiend, and Hellana was a woman with good reason to take threats seriously. Those to herself. And to the child asleep on her shoulder.

"What kind of danger?" She also took a step, closing the gap between them. "Don't be vague, Rook the water-drift. Speak plainly."

"Your father's army marches upon your kingdom. Even now, his troops near the border of your lands."

She drew back, her creamy skin blanching even further. "Impossible. He would never."

Sidestepping her denial, he said, "As you know, mounted warriors will arrive first."

She glanced away, likely imagining the warriors in the sky, riding the backs of vipera, great serpent creatures trained from birth to be merciless in battle.

"You must come with me now," Rook insisted.

Holding up a hand, she closed her eyes briefly. "King Malrik has no interest in me." She looked at him again, eyes cool. "You must be mistaken."

He noted that she didn't call him her father. "I'm sorry, my lady." Rook paused. "He does not come for you."

Her expression grew puzzled, so he hurriedly explained. "Malrik is in search of an oracle. A blind seer."

Hellana gasped. "He comes for Ayleen. But why?"

"Please, there is no time. I've only just had the vision, and if you and your people don't flee—"

"Flee." The word seem to insult her, and she pulled herself up. "We will fight."

Risking himself, he approached and took her free hand. "You don't know me, but you recognize me. I am of your people, your homeland, your kin. I swear, I would never lead you astray. So I'm asking you to trust, to believe me when I tell you, the castle must be abandoned by all."

She pulled away. "No."

"I've seen it, so it is certain. Most will perish, and they will die in horrible ways. Malrik's troops are hungry for blood." He inhaled. "And for women. As their queen, your duty is to save them."

She still didn't look convinced.

"Malrik doesn't care about your land or your castle, but he will annihilate your citizens, using them as food and entertainment. If you leave, it will only be temporary. Please, I beg you, take harbor with your people. We will protect you." He used his strongest argument. "And your babe."

"I . . . I . . ." She stuttered and looked about. "By the stars." She scowled and said, "Fine. I don't know why I believe you."

Rook knew why. The waters of Vei Lani ran true in her veins, and she too possessed the skill of perception.

"I must summon my ladies and make ready to travel." She squared her shoulders. "We will pack quickly."

"Only food and water for the journey. And only they should pack." He steeled himself for further argument. "You, your child, and the oracle must come with me. I'm afraid I can take no more."

Hellana looked him up and down as if he'd offered to roast his eyes for her dinner. "Through the water? I will not risk my child's life."

"We will be in Vei Lani before he has time to draw a single breath. Now go. Give your orders and send for the blind seer. Tell your men to take the route through the—"

"The Bittervald. Yes, I know." Hellana jiggled her small son, now waking in response to her distress. "My mother secreted away instructions for me, in case I ever had to escape Malrik."

Escape her own father? Rook's damp skin ran cold. The one sad statement made him wonder what her childhood had been like.

He cleared his throat and said, "Please, make haste." He gestured up to the sun, climbing toward its Zenith. "Your people must lose themselves in the Bittervald by midday."

Hellana inclined her head sharply. "I'll make sure of it. Then I'll return." Whirling away, she darted across the courtyard.

Rook watched her go, trying to catch his breath and slow his pulse. "And I'll be waiting."

# 8

Sami crossed Main Street, glancing up at the tall brick building with the old clock face hanging high above. As she stepped onto the sidewalk, she glanced up, and a proud smile flitted to her face. Just as it did every time she read the words carved into the wooden sign above the door.

Teal-colored letters in script spelled *The Sweetery*. Such a simple name for Fiona's biggest dream.

Sami stepped inside, and paused, taking a deep, indulgent sniff of whatever glory her little sister had recently baked. And it was as if she'd walked into a homespun dream. A cheerful setting accompanied the tantalizing smells. Wood floors gleamed a soft golden brown, pairing nicely with light walls and accents of pink and the same blueish-green gracing the sign out front. Sami's artistic eye also appreciated the whimsical curves of wrought-iron chairs and matching tables the color of cream.

Hand on her now-grumbling stomach, Sami eased to the glass case, visually devouring every single option. She'd been summoned by Tate for a sisterly pow-wow, the time set well after the morning rush for bagels and donuts but before the lunch crowd trickled in for dessert.

While being pulled from work might be an annoyance, Sami couldn't complain about the designated meeting spot. "Are those chocolate croissants?" she asked, tapping the glass as Fiona turned from a high-end machine with a tiny white cup in her hand. The extra-early routine of the new business had turned her into an espresso junkie.

"Cocoa-hazelnut crème," Fiona said and sipped. "It's dee-lish, if I do say so myself." She wiggled her backside and scrunched up her shoulders. 'Have I told you how much I love this place?"

Sami looked into her sister's bright eyes, and warm affection flooded her heart. "You have, but that's okay. Say it every day if you want. You deserve it." She gestured to the almost-empty boxes behind the glass. "Judging by your low inventory, I'd say everyone in town loves this place."

She sent Fiona a sidelong glance. "You sure you aren't sprinkling magick dust in your recipes?"

"I'll never tell." Fiona winked before grabbing a regular-size mug from a rack and placing it beneath the silver spout of the espresso machine. "A macchiato?" she tossed over her shoulder.

"You know it," Sami said. Her sister wasn't the only one with a new java addiction. "There's only one problem with that contraption."

"What?" Fiona said absently, focused on her task.

"It's too far away from my house. I've been working since six this morning and could have used a pick-me-up about an hour ago." She wrinkled her nose at the memory. "I had to settle for the instant stuff I make."

Fiona pivoted, a surprised but silent "Oh" rounding her mouth. "You've been up since six?"

"Stop telling tall tales, Fee." Tate strolled in from the kitchen, obviously having come in the back way. "Because no one would believe Sami got up that early."

"Hey. I have a work ethic." Sami rolled with her sister's teasing and accepted the dark espresso with a "mark" of milk, hence the name "macchiato." She sipped carefully, judging the heat. It was perfect. "I just employ said ethic when the time is right."

She'd never been on the same timetable as her sisters. Tate and

Fiona both rose early to meet the day and bang out the bulk of their work before lunch. Inspiration dictated Sami's schedule, and she could never be certain when it would strike.

"I know," Tate said, "and you just keep on doing what you do. The pieces you displayed at the show you and Jack had. . ." She trailed off and shook her head. "If I had a fraction of the talent you both do, I'd have a gallery in Paris. Or maybe Rome. Live the decadent life of a Bohemian artist."

Sami rolled her eyes. "Without Jack and your view of the water?"

Tate made a dismissive sound. "Of course not. Jack would go with me, and we'd keep the place here as a summer home." Tate tossed up her hands and beamed at the ceiling. "We'd be all the rage."

Tate was joking, but still Sami asked, "Why don't you? Jack is certainly good enough, and his woodwork would be a hit anywhere."

A little faraway grin curved Tate's lips. "Because I'm home now, and I don't want to leave it again."

She shared a glance with Sami, one that spoke volumes about the journey their relationship had taken. Tate had once fled Bar Harbor, breaking Jack's heart in the process. As well as Sami's, who hadn't understood why her big sister had deserted them all.

She knew now, though. She understood that, as the eldest, Tate had missed their mother most of all. The mother they'd believed dead for so long.

Until the goddess sent them on a quest and changed their lives forever. The sisters had discovered their own magick, and then they'd found their mother, trapped in a Fae prison of glass, sleeping peacefully in the caverns below the family home.

Sami shook off the reverie and looked at her sisters. So much had changed, and all for the better. They both radiated with happiness.

A sudden pang of melancholy crept along the underside of the delight she felt for her sisters. A feeling of longing that swirled down from her chest to weigh heavily in her stomach.

Frowning into her cup, she disregarded the strange ache and decided to chalk it up to hunger. "For the love of Christmas, would you give me one of those croissants?" Mouth watering, she reached for a napkin. "One of the new ones with the hazelnut cream stuff."

With a perky step, Fiona reached under the glass counter and used metal tongs to grab the pastry. "Anything for you, Tate?"

"Yes. I mean, no." Tate scowled at the tempting array of culinary pleasures. "Oh, hell. Give me a cinnamon roll." She put a hand on one hip and moved to the silver machine, proceeding to make herself an Americano. Espresso and hot water, a straightforward drink, and so very Tate-like.

Fiona snatched an apple tartlet for herself, and the three of them silently took a few bites of their respective treats. Sami finished first, washing down the last with a swig of caffeinated bliss.

"Okay." She pushed away her plate, propped one arm on the counter, and cocked the opposite hip. She hated to dampen the mood, but she suspected the reason she'd been called here and wanted to get the conversation over with.

Settling a bored gaze on Tate, she said, "You wanted to talk?"

Unable to speak with her mouth full, Tate bobbed her head. At last, she gulped down the bite. "Don't you think we should?"

Sami shrugged carelessly. "Sure. I thought we finished this yesterday, but let's hear it."

Tate and Fiona exchanged a look, one that told Sami they'd been talking about her. Fiona cleared her throat. "We think it's a good idea to work with Grayson and his company."

"Company?" Sami wiped at the corner of her mouth where it still felt a little sticky. "Such a benign term for organized vampire hunters."

"Does it really matter what we call them?" Tate groused as she put her hand on the counter.

She and Fiona both stood on the opposite side, and Sami

couldn't help feeling ganged up on. "Look, you two have obviously already decided something, so just spit it out."

"We only talked this morning." Fiona rushed to reassure her. "When Tate called me."

"Minutes before I called you, Sami." Tate tapped her nails on the glass. "We aren't keeping you out of the loop, but we're both a little concerned about your behavior lately." She widened her eyes and rolled them to the side. "Especially yesterday."

"Hey, someone had to safeguard our family, since the rest of you all but opened your arms to what could easily have been a wolf in sheep's clothing."

Fiona laughed suddenly, then had a coughing fit. "Don't make me choke, Sami." She giggled again and grinned. "Grayson didn't strike me as anything in sheep's clothing. I think he bared his fangs from the get-go."

"Yes." Tate jumped in. "And promptly attacked *our* enemy."

"So that automatically makes him our friend?" Sami lifted a hand and dropped it, frustrated by her logical sister's completely illogical leap.

"It's a pretty good start," Tate said. "I've been weighing this all out, thinking it over, and we'd be foolish not to accept his help. He's been doing this a lot longer than we have, and the problem clearly reaches farther than our little glass bubble."

"Glass bubble?" Now Sami nearly choked, irritation turning swiftly to outrage. "Someone is *dead*. A college kid who was too young to die had every ounce of blood sucked from his body." She curled her fingers when she felt them tremble. "I think our bubble is well and truly shattered."

The harsh words left a bitter taste on her tongue, and she was shocked by her own burst of temper.

Pressing her lips together, she stared at Tate, preparing for her sister's wrath.

But Tate seemed calm. Patient and—*Oh, no.*

She all but reeked of sympathy.

Sami would prefer to have Tate rip her to shreds. "You know I'm right," Sami spat out, facing Fiona in hope of support.

But there was no help to be found there. Fee tilted her head and looked at Sami as if she were a lost puppy. "We're worried about you, Sami. You're carrying too heavy a burden on your shoulders."

Sami hissed and turned away.

"You are. And you shouldn't bear it by yourself." Tate extended her hand and squeezed Sami's elbow, the only part of her within reach. "The three of us started this thing together. We all chose to go forward, each and every step of the way."

Sami just stared at the back hallway and the cutesy-café-style picture on the wall at the end. If she just ignored them . . .

"You feel guilty for taking the ring," Fiona said. "You blame yourself for bringing the Iele here." She released a heavy sigh. "And that makes me feel even more guilty than you."

Sami whipped her head around. "What? Why?"

Fiona dropped her shoulders. "Because you never would have been there that night to grab the ring if I hadn't wanted to go to the Ielonaar Realm."

"Fee," Sami said, facing her sisters and gripping the edge of the counter with both hands, "you had no way of knowing what would happen, and it's stupid to feel guilty about things you can't control."

When Fiona bit her bottom lip as if she were about to cry, Sami spoke faster. "You went there to save a baby. You only did what you thought was right."

A satisfied gleam entered Fiona's green eyes, and her lips now turned up in a way that could only be described as smug.

"Oh." The steam whooshed out of Sami like a radiator with its cap jerked off. She couldn't help but grin back at her sweet—and *sneaky*—sister. "I see what you did there."

Tate clapped her hands softly. "Bravo, Fee."

Fiona daintily sipped her espresso. "I have my moments."

"Yeah, yeah." Sami slid her empty cup across the glass. "How about another?" she asked, hoping to sidetrack at least one of her sisters while she mulled over the point Fiona had so cleverly made.

Had Sami been doing what she'd thought was right when she'd grabbed the ring? She couldn't be sure. So much had happened so fast, and all they'd wanted was to get the child to safety.

But when she'd seen the ring, when she'd imagined its power in the hands of Malrik . . .

Her mind was all muddled now, and she wasn't sure what made her feel worse. The fact that she'd brought magickal jewelry back home and vampires along with it, or that she'd stewed about it so much and acted out enough to make her sisters worry.

And if they had worried, so had her mother and grandfather. And Brit. And maybe Kat, who didn't need the added stress with her pregnancy. Sami's head started to hurt, the ache spreading down her jaw and into her neck.

"Will you stop, already?" Tate slapped her arm. "I can see you winding yourself up again. I'll say this clearly, so listen up. You. Should. Not. Feel. Guilty." She punctuated each word with a thrust of her pointed finger.

Sami sucked in a breath and imagined drawing all of her emotions down with it. She obviously needed to work on being less transparent. "How do you know it's guilt?"

Tate made a face just as Fiona returned with the drink and said, "That's right. For all we know, she could be worked up over a man."

Sami was truly baffled. "A man? Who has the time?" In fact, she hadn't had a date since . . . Well, she had to think for a second. Then a lightbulb went off.

She'd had virtually zero social engagements since they'd all returned from the Iele farworld. With the ring. The damned ring that was ruining her life.

"No, it's not that," Sami grumbled. "With all that's been

happening, I've been too pre-occupied to go out with anyone."

"Oh, I know that." Fiona leveled a direct gaze at her. "But I don't think it's a man you've *already* been out with that's creating the problem."

"What problem?" Sami asked.

"*Ohhh.*" Tate nodded slowly. "I did pick up on that."

"You, too?" Fiona asked innocently, putting a finger to her chin.

"Picked up on what?" Sami demanded, growing agitated again.

"She *has* been extra-grouchy the last couple of days." Tate spoke as if Sami weren't even in the room.

Fiona slid her gaze back to Sami. "And by her own admission, she thinks he's handsome."

"Who?" Sami asked, crossing her arms in self-defense. "I haven't said that about anyone. Not lately."

Fiona's jaw dropped and she let out a squeak. "Sami, it was literally the first thing you ever said to him." Fiona dropped her voice to mimic Sami. "Well, you're a handsome one, aren't you?"

Comprehension finally dawned, and Sami's immediate response was, "Oh, *hell* no." Arms still crossed, she sent an extra-hot glare at both of her siblings. "You have both lost your minds."

"Oh, yeah?" Tate hiked a single brow in challenge. "I guess we'll just see about that."

"No. Uh-uh. No way." Sami shook her head decisively. "And why would we?"

"Because," Tate jerked her chin toward the front of the shop and grinned, "Mr. Handsome is about to walk through that door."

# 9

"Don't say anything about the ring." Apprehension clutched at Sami as soon as she spied Grayson through the door's glass. She couldn't say why he sent a cascade of fight-or-flight sensations through her veins, but her spine shot straight as a lance, and her heart felt like it stretched to full capacity before collapsing in on itself with a dull thud.

Grimacing, she used two fingers to rub the spot in her chest where she felt the aftershocks, reverberations caused by Grayson-induced stress.

As she willed away the mild discomfort, Sami wondered how her sisters could ever imagine she had a thing for the guy. With a huff, she crossed her arms—as if to ward off the very idea—and watched him open the door to cross the threshold.

"Morning, Grayson," Fiona chimed out.

And made Sami tense up all over.

Grayson strode through the sweet shop with total confidence, almost as if he owned the place. While Tate and Fiona beamed at him like a couple of idiots.

Sami barely held back a snort. So much for witches having a sixth sense. Shifting, she tossed her sisters a heated glare, but neither of them paid any heed.

What was wrong with them? Why weren't they more guarded?

Love, she thought with a purse of her lips. That was the answer. Newfound romances had clearly addled her sisters' brains. Otherwise, they'd see Grayson for what he was—a hard, emotionless man on a mission.

And just what would happen when the mission was over? Once he'd teased out all the information he wanted, would that single-minded focus be turned on her family? His secret society exterminated vampires, so what was their policy on humans with power?

His "company" might also consider magic a threat, and for all Sami knew, the Whiteburn name was already on a kill list.

So she'd watch. She'd monitor. And she'd be ready, if needed, to defend them all.

With an amiable grin for Fiona and Tate, Grayson moved to the counter. He spoke briefly with them both, all smiles and charm as they discussed the glorious weather.

Then his critical eyes landed on Sami.

She would swear she heard their stares clash, an audible sound of steel meeting stone. Aloof, but alert, she inclined her head in greeting. "LeRoux." Her voice lacked Fiona's enthusiasm, and she used his last name on purpose, avoiding any hint of friendship. "I'm surprised to see you here. Out for a morning cupcake?"

If he noticed the dig to his masculinity, he gave no indication as he peered into the display case. "I wouldn't say no to one. Everything in here looks delicious." He gestured to the far left side. "But especially those cupcakes."

Sliding a smirk toward Sami, he added, "The ones with little pink flowers."

So he *had* noticed. Point for the visiting team.

Though she and Grayson seemed to be the only ones competing.

Well, that was fine by her. She would happily go head-to-head with the cocky intruder. Tate and Fiona might be dazzled by the nice-guy routine, but she saw right past the charm and straight to the tiny bulge on the side of his rigid jaw.

He was on edge, just like Sami. Because like her, he still had doubts.

"Actually," he said, dropping all pretense of cheeriness and refocusing on Fiona and Tate, "I came by for a reason. I wanted to ask about Kat, to see if she's feeling better. And," he said in a no-bullshit tone, "if she learned anything more about your friend, Rook."

The muscles in his shoulders tightened, almost imperceptibly, but Sami discerned the slightest bit of tension. Was he honestly concerned about Kat, or just paving his way?

"She's fine," Tate assured him. "Surprised and shaken up, which is understandable. But, no. She hasn't learned anything new."

"I hope you'll let me know if she does." Grayson glanced outside as two laughing women passed by. "Or if any of you encounter more Iele. Even the good ones," he said with meaning.

"You wouldn't hurt him, though," Fiona said, crunching her brows down. "If we tell you Rook is a friend, you'll take our word." In one swift move, sweet baby Fee morphed into a protective witch to be treated with caution.

Inside, Sami cheered.

"I said we'd work together, and I meant it." Grayson spoke firmly but without resentment. "However, your friend could be an important source, and we need to gather as much intel as possible."

Fiona considered his words, and her expression softened, flickering back to that of the pleasant shopkeeper. "Alright, then. So," she spread her hands to indicate the goods, "what can I get you?"

Hands on hips, Grayson perused the wares, paying special attention to Fiona's trademark pastries, recipes she'd created herself.

Despite the innocuous topic, his posture still reminded Sami of the military, of a soldier honed into a deadly weapon, fierce and focused only on his duty. By his own admission, he'd been trained since childhood, taught to track and hunt. Taught to kill.

Even the polo shirt—hugging his torso quite nicely—didn't disguise the sense of danger he exuded. His collar lay open, exposing what appeared to be the edge of a tattoo on tanned skin.

Sami's fingers itched to peel back the fabric, to discover what a man like him would have forever imprinted on his flesh.

As he continued to chat with Fiona about her shop, Sami studied their would-be collaborator. LeRoux, she thought, mentally rolling the name around. She could see the French in him, eyes a few shades deeper than the average brown and fringed with the kind of lashes that made female hearts patter.

Sami might be contrary, and definitely suspicious, but she was still a woman. And she wasn't blind. So yeah, she allowed, he was a good-looking man.

If you liked the broody, tough-guy type.

His raven hair was the only thing not fitting the military mold, too long for a soldier, falling onto his forehead. She was lost in her musings, wondering if he was simply overdue for a cut, when he stepped closer for a better look at the bagels.

And the scent of just-showered male eclipsed that of baked goods.

Sami only caught a trace. A single whiff of clean, crisp man. But her skin prickled, her blood flowed hot, and the involuntary response she felt wasn't fight. Or flight.

Shocked by the tingling warmth unfurling in her stomach, she took two quick steps backward. Pretending she simply wanted her coffee, she whisked her cup from the countertop.

Only a swallow remained, but she lifted it to her mouth and inhaled deeply, masking the cologne, or body wash—or whatever the hell he wore that smelled so good.

Two parallel lanes of sensation ran through her—one of distrust, one of lust. The sensations did not mesh well together.

And *damned* if she'd tell her sisters.

Sipping the last bit of her drink, she waved the mug at Tate. In a rough voice she asked, "Would you make me another?" Anything to keep her mind off of the man who continued to find new and unexpected ways to annoy her.

Gathering her loose curls together, Sami pulled a band from her pocket and tied back her hair, using the act as an excuse to keep her gaze on the floor. She had nothing to worry about, or feel guilty over. So she'd had a momentary lapse. So what? She'd experienced a perfectly normal male-female chemical reaction, and only for a few seconds.

By the time Tate handed her the macchiato and gave her a wink, Sami had almost succeeded in talking herself down. It was no big deal. Nothing permanent. And most importantly, no one ever had to know.

It's not liked she'd jumped the guy on one of Fiona's little white tables.

Satisfied with her rationale and returned to normal, she angled toward Grayson. No matter what she saw, heard—or smelled—she was determined to be made of marble. Utterly unflinching. Nonreactive.

And then she looked out to the sidewalk and saw two men. Two huge, hulking, intimidating men.

*Grayson's* men.

Eyes narrowed, she motioned to the brutes with her cup. "Why are your guys here, LeRoux? They like cupcakes, too?" She smirked when his jaw clenched even harder. "Or do you just feel the need for backup?"

"Not at all." Grayson faced her without sparing a glance outside. Instead, his gaze dipped briefly. His right eye twitched. Then his stare penetrated her again. "Because I don't consider you a threat."

~~~

When Sami's nostrils flared in response, Grayson reminded

himself he shouldn't prod her, not when that glorious temper always seemed to be sizzling just below the surface. But he'd had to say something, even a comment meant to irritate.

Better to risk getting her riled up than have her realize he'd been looking at her legs.

He'd sensed her eyes on him moments before, like heat stroking over his skin. That had been bad enough, but then she'd turned and stepped to the counter, the move drawing his attention down. Down to long, long legs, tight and toned with the perfect amount of summer glow.

Not to mention her khaki shorts, ones that were almost too snug for comfort. For his comfort, anyway.

But he'd only jumped from one danger zone into another, since staring at her face didn't solve the problem. Fury flashed within her eyes. In that pure, undiluted brown that made him think of the bayou, of the deep, dark, and secret places. Where it was both easy and pleasurable for a man to get lost.

Wary of sinking in any further, he tore his stare from Sami and diverted himself to safer and more solid ground. To Fiona and Tate. "I wanted to speak with the three of you."

Tate held up a finger. "Okay, but first, how do you take your coffee?"

"Black. Thanks."

"One Americano coming up." Tate placed a mug beneath a spouted machine and got to work, just as a woman entered the store with a red-headed little girl in a purple leotard and tutu. Fiona greeted them, chatted briefly, and set about filling a white box with pastel-frosted cookies.

Grateful for the reprieve, Grayson reeled himself back in and avoided looking at Sami. He had to get his shit together. Sami Whiteburn was hardly the first woman he'd ever spent time with or worked alongside. Hell, he'd sparred and wrestled with plenty of lookers over the years. And not once had he lost focus or forgotten his purpose.

Not like he'd found himself doing the last thirty-six hours. The approximate amount of time since a certain curly-haired witch had tried to light him up.

Hearing excited babbling, Grayson turned to watch the little girl bounce on her toes as she told of the party her dance class was having after today's practice. Her sweet face and happy smile lanced straight through him. Helped him re-center.

He had no business thinking of Sami in any way other than as a colleague. Emotion merited no place in his line of work, and desire could be an unhealthy distraction. Especially when people's lives were at risk.

The sound of Tate setting the hot drink before him snapped him back. After murmuring his thanks, he sipped the brew until the mother and daughter exited the shop with their cookies.

Alone again with the Whiteburns, he held a single-mindedness, a determination to get back to business. He positioned himself so he could see all three women and gauge their reactions to what he had to say. "My men and I went down to the harbor today, and I noticed a disturbance in the water. A strange residue, with a slight glimmer."

The sisters shared brief glances but didn't respond.

"Definitely not of human origin." He paused. Still nothing.

He took another casual drink of coffee before releasing a breath. "Why don't you meet me halfway and confirm what I already know?" Then, employing a basic interrogation method, he let the question hang in the air. And waited.

Surprisingly, Sami was the first to speak. "You probably found the place where Rook came out of the water. I'm guessing your *heightened senses*," she gave a slight curl of her lip, "led you to where he entered our world."

Hiding the shock the news caused him, Grayson stared at her with lasered focus. "He came from the ocean? Just exited the water to arrive here?"

Sami performed a nod-and-shrug combo.

Pretending his body hadn't hardened from top to bottom, he said, "You don't seem worried that an Iele can come here so easily."

"Rook is not a concern. He's not a danger." Tate answered him, standing straighter as her expression tightened. "On that, you'll just have to take our word."

"And the ability to travel that way is very rare, even for his kind." Fiona tossed out the statement while blithely reorganizing the cookie display.

Grayson studied the trio, their expressions ranging from blasé to barely concerned. The only concern they had was probably for him, and how he would respond to the news. Why did he get the feeling they were more worried about his presence than a foreign and deadly species invading their town?

Shaking his head, he walked away from the counter. Then he circled back. After all the years he'd spent tracking and exterminating Iele offspring, learning the originals could return with so little effort shook him to the core.

And yet, the news had been delivered so casually.

How many Iele had come to Bar Harbor? Had there been a change in their realm? Some sort of disaster that drove them here to scout the resources?

Or food sources. Like a world full of warm-blooded humans.

In a rare show of frustration, Grayson raked a hand through his hair. "You need to tell me about all the Iele you've come into contact with, including Rook. Why did he come here? What makes you think he means no harm?"

"We don't think. We know," Sami said. "We're positive, because Kat said so."

"Fine. So how can *she* be so sure?" Grayson would swear he felt the vein in his forehead pulse.

Sami looked to her sister. "Tate, why don't you take this one?"

"Alright." Tate sighed, and with a neutral expression, began her timeline a few months earlier, in the spring. She explained how Rook had arrived suddenly and approached Kat in her candle shop.

When Tate pointed, Grayson spared a glance to the store on the corner across the street.

"At first, she thought he would hurt her," Tate explained. "I'll tell you that honestly. But he didn't. In fact, he intervened when Kat and Brit were attacked by one of King Malrik's followers. Rook saved Kat's life that night, and they . . ." Here her gaze slid to the side in thought. "Well, they formed a connection. Kat is intuitive. She's a water witch."

"And Rook came from the water." Grayson took a guess and received a nod in the affirmative.

Tate continued her story, explaining how Rook and Kat had joined their gifts to "look" into Malrik's world. She insisted Rook was an ally, and that he bore no good will toward King Malrik.

Still unsettled, Grayson mulled over the details. "So you're saying Malrik is the only problem, the only danger, not just for us but for Rook as well. All because the king wants some mysterious relic he thinks you three can help him find."

He rubbed his jaw, disturbed by the idea of Iele drama spilling over into his world. Centuries had gone by with no originals being sighted, and now they were popping up like an epidemic.

"What would you do?" Sami demanded.

He jerked his attention to her. "What do you mean?"

She edged closer. "If you and Rook came face to face, what would you do?"

Grayson moved as well, closing the gap until they were separated by only a couple of feet. "My job," he answered plainly. "I'd assess the risk."

"Even though we've told you he's a friend?" She crossed her arms, essentially throwing up a barricade. "Would this assessment come before or after you put a blade through his heart?"

Grayson ground his jaw, refusing to give her what she so clearly wanted. Another fight. But at this point, he couldn't offer her any assurances either. His whole life had been dedicated to destroying Iele, and the testimony of three witches couldn't change that overnight.

He wanted to develop this alliance, but he wouldn't give her false promises.

So they glared at each other, locked in a battle of wills.

Then Sami's gaze shifted. She looked past him, her scowl deepening. "Fee," she called. "What are you doing?"

Grayson followed her line of sight to see Fiona taking two large muffins out the door. She said something to Finley and Dodge who were both still waiting outside. Then she handed them each a muffin, earning huge, grateful grins from each.

Grayson drew a deep breath and spoke in a low voice. "They aren't going to hurt her, Sami."

"How can I be sure of that? It's clear you don't trust us."

A sarcastic chuckle rumbled free before he could stop it. "And your well of trust runs so deep."

She frowned, started to speak, but stopped abruptly when Fiona appeared beside them. "Okay, everything is set for tomorrow night."

For once, Sami and Grayson were on the same page, both casting Fiona looks of confusion. "What happens tomorrow night?" Sami asked.

"We all go out to dinner. Get to know each other over steak and lobster." Fiona tapped her chin. "Or burritos. Whatever gets the vote." She waved to Finley and Dodge through the large front window. The two men—both with a background in the vampire equivalent of special ops—waved back like Fiona's oldest and dearest friends.

"Your team." Fiona hooked a thumb toward the men before

waving a finger to indicate herself and her sisters. "Our team." She gave a decisive nod. "Breaking bread together is an age-old custom when it comes to creating alliances."

"I don't think—" Sami began, but snapped her mouth closed when Fiona's eyes widened and she put her hands on her hips. "Okay, okay. Geez." Sami put up her hands but maintained her unhappy expression. "At least we'll be in a public place."

"Right," Grayson said, picking up her cynicism and running with it. "And that means no flame-throwing allowed."

Sami just grunted.

And he had to smile.

He liked the plan, though, certain a union with the witches would aid his endeavors, his intent to stop the stream of incoming Iele. So when Fiona clasped her hands, declaring, "This will be good," Grayson tilted his head toward Sami and uttered, "I can't wait."

And meant it.

# 10

Royal Palace of Vei Lani
The Ielonaar Realm

Hellana woke to bright sunlight and the ever-present lullaby of waves rolling ashore. Though stillness filled her chamber in the Vei Lanian palace, she eased quietly to the bassinet near her bed. Keaghan slept peacefully, a tiny fist pressed to his cheek, his dark tuft of hair showing the slightest glint of blue.

The flood of affection almost took her breath away, as it did most mornings when she saw him again. The burst of love was followed by a sense of contentment, and of wonder. Feelings she had yet to grow accustomed to, even after all these months.

After gazing at his little face a moment longer, she left her child to his rest and moved to the tall windows, their sheer white drapes billowing in the air. Air scented with the salt of the sea and blooms of orelia, the large golden flowers trailing in vines down the walls of the palace.

She leaned out to appreciate the plants, amazed by how different this place was from her own lands, those she'd ruled since Emuirdane's death. Savoring the warmth of the sun, she allowed herself a short time to observe, to enjoy the guileless beauty that was Vei Lani.

After years of being the "strange one" in exotic clothes, it pleased her to see so many women dressed as she normally was, with bare midriffs and gauzy skirts. But in addition to the range of blues she preferred, the locals used accents of bright pinks, yellows, and greens—all happy colors and properly befitting the joyous people.

A tickle of what might have been pride started in her throat, then spread to lift her lips and sting her eyes.

This was her homeland. Her kin. Her culture.

Over the years, she'd often wondered how her mother—reportedly a kind, cheerful young woman—had fallen in love with the beast that was Hellana's father. Yes, she'd also heard how her mother's death had devastated Malrik, how loss and fury had changed him, but no reason or excuse could ever garner her forgiveness.

How might her life have been different, Hellana wondered, if her mother hadn't died in childbirth? If her death hadn't also killed every ounce of Malrik's love?

He'd been a neglectful father at best, his hate-filled stares and cruel words the only attention given to his small daughter. Until the day he'd found a use for her. The day he'd bartered her into marriage, trading her life and freedom to Emuirdane, in exchange for the Jeweled Ceffyl.

But all for nothing, as it turned out. Ironic, in the end, that her father had killed Emuirdane, thus releasing her from the prison to which he'd once banished her.

She glanced back at her sleeping son, vowing to never let her own needs rise above his. From the moment she'd felt the first little flutter in her belly, Hellana had known true love. Love that had filled her with light and clarity, chasing away the hate she'd once clung to.

Her baby hadn't been just a miracle, but also her salvation.

After his birth, she'd looked hard at herself and had worked to change. That change meant admitting the horrible things she'd done in the past. But also admitting that she too had been a victim, raised with loathing and taught only rage.

Malrik's rage. A black evil that hounded her still.

"Tisu!" a light voice called out from below.

The bright sound danced in the air and pulled Hellana from her musings. She looked to find a little girl in a dress the color of stars and sky. The child hopped up and down, waving her hand.

Surprise jolted Hellana, and she almost looked behind her.

But the child continued to wave, eyes intent on the woman in the window. Now she used both hands. "Tisu," she cried out again, her smile wide and friendly.

Hellana suddenly remembered. Tisu was an old word, an ancient Vei Lanian greeting. Loosely translated, it meant "beautiful welcome." She'd learned of the expression while researching her ancestors from her mother's lineage. Now here she was, hearing for herself.

And the small gesture touched her deeply.

She lifted her hand in acknowledgement, and with a giggle, the girl bounded away. She ran to the beach and joined a woman who strolled in the surf. A mother and daughter, enjoying the freedom and beauty of a peaceful land.

That's what I want for my boy, she told herself. Freedom and peace.

A knock sounded on the door, and Hellana swung around. She hurried to a chaise covered in ice-blue velvet and retrieved the dressing robe she'd been provided. "A moment," she called out, wrapping herself quickly to prepare for company. "You may enter."

The handsome face she was beginning to know well popped inside the open door. "Your Highness," Rook said, "may I have a word?"

"Of course. Please." She motioned him inside.

"I have news," he said, bowing his head slightly. "Your people have been spotted. The convoy has crossed the border into our lands."

Relief swamped her, a release of heavy worry. And a much

greater load than she'd realized she carried. "My people are safe."

"Yes, and we almost have the buildings ready to house them. Our barracks have gone unused for many years, but they have been cleaned and are being readied as we speak."

"You have been more than generous." The gratitude she felt was warm and true. "Thank you."

"You are most welcome, Your Highness."

"Please, you should call me Hellana. Your uncle is king here, so you also have royal blood. I believe we can do away with such stifling formality." She conjured a smile. "Between friends."

"As you wish," he said, slanting a single brow and offering a grin in return, one that sparked an odd yet pleasant burn in her stomach.

Which she staunchly ignored.

"We have rooms here for your nurse, Veloria, as well as her sister. Both will be made comfortable, their chambers only around the corner from you."

Though Hellana didn't view Veloria or Ayleen as servants, she was stunned that they would be housed within the palace. "That is gracious of you." The benevolence of Rook and his people continued to humble her.

*Benevolence.* A trait she'd tried to embody in recent months. And yet, in the face of such gentle humanity, she still felt unworthy. Unclean. As if the sins of both her husband and her father marked her flesh for the entire realm to see.

She turned quickly to stare out the window again.

"What's wrong?" Rook asked.

Hellana regretted her rush of emotion, something she could never hope to hide from an intuitive with his power.

"Was it something I said?"

"No, no." Turning back to him, Hellana clasped her hands together and squeezed.

"Your Highness." He stepped to her, his hand falling gently to her arm. "Hellana."

There was that scintillating burn again, and this time, it couldn't be ignored. Bemused by her reaction, she gazed down at his fingers resting lightly above her elbow.

He quickly pulled away. "My apologies. I shouldn't take such liberties." His voice held censure, for himself.

Hellana couldn't bear the sound of it.

"No, it's not that. It's only that you are the first man to touch me since . . ." she couldn't say the bastard's name, "my husband's death. And I'll tell you," she added softly, "yours is the first that doesn't cause me to flinch."

Even when he'd wrapped his arms around her and Keaghan, transporting them through the water, she'd been unafraid. And he'd kept his promise, delivering them to a dark pond high in the Vei Lanian hills, before her baby could draw a single breath.

Then he'd carried her child down the winding trail, moving with such caution on the steeper slopes.

Hellana took his fingers in hers. "I owe you much, Rook. And I do not fear you."

After a lifetime without love, only knowing greed, possession, and cruelty at the hands of men—of *family*—how could the tiny seed of trust he'd planted have already blossomed? Why did seeing him enter the room instill her with a sense of calm, and of safety?

"I don't know what to think of you," she told him honestly. "Your kindness is unending, and normally I would be suspicious. I would question your motives."

"But you don't," he said plainly.

"But I don't." She shrugged. "And for reasons I can't understand, that makes me feel . . . unbalanced," she said. Though *terrified* is what she thought. Yet hopeful.

And it was the burgeoning hope that also brought the fear.

"Hellana," he said, releasing her name slowly, almost tenderly. "After what you've endured, your faith in me is a true gift. And I think I'd like to be considered a friend."

He tightened his hold on her hand before letting go and taking a step in retreat. "I'd be happy to escort you to the evening meal and introduce you to my family." He tilted his head, eyes alight as he added, "And to yours."

"My family?" The air in her lungs froze. "My grandparents have passed."

"Yes, but you have an aunt and cousins."

"An aunt?" Her knees gave, but Rook swooped in to support her. He guided her to the chaise.

Glad to be seated, Hellana melted into the plush fabric. She pressed a hand to a heart that felt too weak. "I never knew my mother had a sister."

"I'm sorry." Rook kneeled before her. "I didn't know."

"How could you?" The shock slowly filtered from Hellana's system. "It seems I must offer my thanks again." Her delight bloomed into a smile. "And you said I have cousins?"

"Yes. They are eager to see you and have been given seats of honor for tonight's feast." His grin faltered as he grew pensive. "But . . ."

"But what?" Hellana asked, the light of her joy dimming.

"The council, our governing body, has called for an assembly. They have questions for you."

"About my father," she guessed, her gut churning as worries returned. Would she be judged for the sins of others? Malrik's blood ran in her veins, as Emuirdane's ran in her child's.

She feared facing the good people of this land, yet as a ruler charged with caring for citizens, she understood why she must. "I do have a dark past, and my very presence here could bring danger."

Not her presence, she silently corrected, but that of Ayleen. Veloria's sister, the blind oracle Malrik sought to find.

"I will speak with them," Hellana said, rising.

Rook stood as well.

"I will offer any help I can," she told him. "You and your people have shown such hospitality."

"Hellana, I promise you—" A knock on the door interrupted whatever Rook had been about to say. He glanced over his shoulder and moved to open the door. "I had breakfast sent up, if that's all right."

"Of course." Hellana watched as a young Vei Lanian male with lighter blue hair carried in a tray and placed it on a white oval table. Only then did she notice the legs had been carved into what must have been some sort of sea creatures with curling tails to create the feet.

Rook excused the young man and lifted the silver dome covering the food. "It's a typical Vei Lanian breakfast, but if there's something you'd rather have, please tell me."

"No, it's fine." She edged closer and pointed to a soft fruit, its pale orange skin reminding her of the dawn. "But what is that?"

"That is a sangrine, native only to our lands. A favorite among the ladies." He sent her a sidelong glance. "I'm betting you will love it."

"I'm sure I will." She studied the tray with two cooked eggs presented in small silver holders, a small round loaf of fresh bread, and a variety of butters and fruit toppings to choose from. Along with small bowls of puree she expected were for Keaghan. "It's wonderful, Rook. Thank you."

"I'll return in two hours and take you to the council hall. And don't worry." His eyes, blue as the ocean's depths, held fast to hers. "I'll be at your side the entire time."

Not trusting herself to speak over the strange lump in her throat, Hellana bowed her head slightly in response. She watched him leave.

Once he'd gone, she picked up the sangrine, colorful and tropical, like Vei Lani.

Taking the fruit with her, Hellana gazed out the open door, across the veranda, and to the bright, open sea. She held the sangrine gently, wondering if her mother had enjoyed the treat as a girl.

With the sun on her face and breeze in her hair, she savored the connection to her mother as she lifted the fruit to her nose.

Sweet and clean, it smelled of freedom.

And of hope.

# 11

Sami stood by as the hostess in her crisp white shirt and black skirt tossed out a brilliant smile. "Whiteburn? Yes, we have you all set up." She gestured to a younger, blonder version of herself. "Tani will take you."

"Thank you," Tate said, setting off after the young woman. Jack walked alongside Tate while Sami and Fiona followed behind.

Sami tucked her hands into the pockets of her pants, surveying the historic hotel and its perfectly groomed gardens. "Nice choice, Fee."

"Thanks." Fiona hunched her shoulders up and then let them fall with a dramatic sigh. "I just love this place."

With its location on Frenchman Bay, the hotel's restaurant did a brisk business, especially in the high-tourist season of summer. Luckily, Fiona had an in with the pastry chef and had gotten a reservation on the patio overlooking the water.

Only a short walk through lupines blooming in lilac and cream and they found the outdoor dining area, candles already shimmering on every table.

They walked across pavers laid in an ashlar pattern beneath honey-colored umbrellas that echoed the vivid sunset. But though the horizon exploded with color, Sami's gaze locked on the tables pushed together to seat seven.

They locked on to Grayson.

Good Southern gentleman that he was, he stood as she and her sisters approached with Jack. The two men with him followed suit.

Fiona took the lead and made introductions. "Finley and Dodge," she said, pointing out each of the muscular men, "this is my sister Sami, and my sister Tate with her husband Jack."

Handshakes and hellos were exchanged, and Finley—red of hair and simply *huge*—used one hand to pull out a chair. "Here you go, Fiona."

"Why, thank you." Sami's younger sister perched herself in the seat and scooted back up as Jack held a chair for Tate before sitting beside her.

Realizing she should have paid attention to the arrangement, Sami had no choice but to edge around to the opposite side of the tables where the only empty spot remained. Right next to Grayson.

"LeRoux," she said, a slight dip of her head in greeting. Calling on her manners, she sat with her back straight and laid the linen napkin over her lap.

If etiquette had to be her shield of choice, then so be it. She had a plan to get her through the potentially awkward evening. A simple plan. One consisting of three easy rules.

She would not butt heads with Grayson. She would not insult Grayson. And she would not treat him like the bastard son returned home to steal her throne.

Tate's words. Not hers.

Though Sami had to admit the analogy rang true.

On the ride over, her sisters had cornered her, essentially ganging up on her to remind her that Grayson and his men were experts on the Iele. That they might actually be helpful in protecting Bar Harbor.

In a very nice but forceful tone, Fiona had told Sami to table whatever suspicions she had and stop looking a gift stallion in the mouth.

Sami released a small *hmph*. Grayson might be tall, strong, and bold—with striking black hair—but Sami rejected the notion of him as a stallion.

Forcing the comparison from her mind, she scanned her menu as the others did theirs, occasionally nodding and joining in while they all made small talk.

Jack recommended those in the mood for a beer try one from the resident brewery, and it wasn't until well after those drinks had been served—with all three visitors trying the local brews— that Dodge set his elbows on the table and threaded his fingers together.

"Now that we're settled in," he said, "I'd love to hear more about your escapades with our long-toothed friends. If you get my meaning," he added with a wink.

Subtle? Not so much. But Sami found herself instantly amenable to the bald-headed man who looked like he could snap a telephone pole over his knee.

"Grayson's told us most of it," the flame-haired Finley put in, "but we're dying to hear more. If you're okay with that."

Sami kept mute. Determined to stick to the plan. To *lie low*.

But when Grayson's knee brushed hers under the table, she jolted, her gaze bouncing off of his as lightning bolts danced from the point of contact up to her thigh.

"Sorry," he mumbled, sitting straighter in his chair.

Sami tried to smile but whatever crossed her face felt more like the grimace of the demented. So she grabbed her Harbor Moon Hops and sucked for dear life.

Why was she so nervous all of a sudden? And why did Grayson seem just as uncomfortable as she was?

Over something as benign as bumped knees?

Ignoring his proximity, she rubbed the tingles out of her leg and forced her mind elsewhere. She let it drift to the soothing sounds of the bay, to creaking boats and harping gulls, tuning out as her sisters and Jack recounted tales of Faerie, the Winter Queen, and the foulest of them all—Emuirdane.

The scent of salty ocean air calmed her, and she tuned back in to Dodge's excited voice. "So you turned the statue into a real horse and set it free?" He tilted his head, his features lit up in awe.

"It's true. I swear." Fiona laughed a little.

"Good job." He gave her a thumbs-up. "I'm an animal lover myself."

"And he's got the T-shirts to prove it." Finley shot his friend a teasing grin. "Tell them about the one with the kittens."

"Bite me. Oh, sorry." Dodge held up his hands and glanced at each of the women.

"Don't worry," Tate assured him, "we've heard, *and said*, much worse."

"And there is no kind of fighting like sister-fighting." Finley widened his eyes. "Believe me, I know. I have three, with tempers to match their ginger hair."

"Ouch," Jack said with sympathy. "So you can imagine these three during their teenage years. Well," he squinted one eye in thought, "mostly Sami and Tate."

"Hey, I could be pretty mean," Fiona objected.

"Oh, like when you would offer us cookies to stop fighting?" Sami said, caught up in the joking and the memories. "You were vicious, Fee." She grinned over the rim of her beer bottle. "Truly vicious."

"I had my moments." Fiona narrowed her green eyes at Sami. "Remember when Tommy Giletti told me he thought you were pretty?"

Sami winced. "Now that you mention it."

"What? What?" Dodge leaned in. "What'd she do?"

Tate slapped fingers to her lips, then forcibly swallowed what she had in her mouth before chortling with laughter. "I forgot about that. Actually, Fiona, you do have at least one vicious bone in your body."

Fiona preened. "Never mess with a twelve-year-old girl's crush."

Sami groaned. "Let's just say little miss Betty Crocker added something extra to my favorite brownies." She envisioned herself pigging out on the treats. "She wrapped them up in cellophane with a red bow and left them in my room."

"Where no one else would find them," Fiona said, covering her face. "Oh, I was horrible."

"Sami was in the bathroom the whole night." Still laughing, Tate put a hand to her stomach. "She even had to skip school the next day."

"Alright, alright." Sami's cheeks started to burn. Way too much information, she decided, darting a look to Grayson.

He was staring back at her. "Back in the day when laxatives came in chocolate form?"

Now her cheeks burst into flame. "Wow. Talk about getting to know someone." Mortified by what the whole table had to be picturing, Sami grabbed her butter knife and started tapping the handle lightly on the table. "We should talk about something else."

Luckily, Fiona swooped in to save her by speaking to Finley and Dodge. "Oh, we didn't tell you about the vipera."

"The what now?" Dodge asked, keenly interested.

"They were so gorgeous." Tate clapped a hand to her heart. "Who would have guessed dragons came in so many bright colors?"

Now Finley almost spit out his drink. "Did you say dragons?"

With the fresh tidbit fueling a new discussion, Sami began to relax again. And only a small bit of humiliation remained by the time servers delivered the main course to the tables.

Lobster bake and pan-seared salmon were the winners all around, except for Sami and Grayson, who'd both ordered the lobster macaroni. "Can't go wrong with mac and cheese." He held his bottle up to toast with hers.

He seemed genuine, so she relented and returned his smile as she clinked her brew against his. "For once, we are in complete agreement."

The casual and amiable vibe resumed as they ate, with talking points centered this time on Bar Harbor and the surrounding area. They discussed the places in town for food and the beauty to be found in Acadia National Park.

"Hopefully we'll have a chance to get out there." Finley pushed back his plate and folded his hands over his belly. "After things have . . . settled down."

Sami started to broach the subject of the danger still looming, but she paused, sensing Grayson's attention. She turned her head and tracked his gaze. Straight down to her hips. "LeRoux," she said under her breath.

Eyes still on her, he reached out.

And Sami jerked in her chair.

Those dark liquid eyes of his jumped to hers. "Can I see your dagger?"

Sami's breath whooshed out. "Uh. My dagger. Yeah. Sure." Fumbling to remove the blade from its sheath, she tried to deny the physical awareness fluttering in her stomach.

"Mine is concealed," he said, studying the weapon. "Didn't think it was legal but, for obvious reasons, I always carry."

"Mine's concealed, too," Sami spit out, unsure why even his small comments put her on the defensive. "It's charmed, so only family and friends can—" Realization had her biting down before she finished the sentence.

What did it mean that the spell she'd cast had determined Grayson to be a friend? It was the only way he could have seen her dagger.

"Charmed? How do you—"

"Never mind. It's complicated." She pressed her lips together, unwilling to admit what her own magick was trying to tell her. "Tell me how yours works."

One black brow lifted in question, but he answered her anyway. "Certainly not by magick. What we have is fairly high-tech with a specialized injection system. Here." He used her blade to demonstrate, drawing a line down the center with his finger.

Acute interest banished her nervousness. "For the gold?"

"Yes. All of our hand-to-hand weapons are designed to release a shot of liquid infused with finely powdered gold. Only a small amount is required to kill, if it enters the bloodstream."

"You weren't lying about being high-tech." Sami nodded, her mind whirring as she imagined the mechanism.

"Yes, our bullets, too. But this," he said in a low voice, running the pads of his fingers over her dagger lovingly. "This is art. Where did you have it made?"

"I made it."

"You did this?" He actually gaped. "How did you get the gold in that marbleized pattern?"

Flattered yet slightly uncomfortable, Sami shrugged. "I used magick."

With an easy move, Grayson reversed the dagger, the sharp end toward himself, and handed the weapon back to Sami. "It really is amazing. You're a true artist."

He'd hit the bullseye without knowing it. "Actually, that's how I make my living. Without the magick part, of course."

"An artist." His eyes gleamed with appreciation, and he lifted one side of his mouth, grinning as if he'd just made a connection. "That explains your passion." Now his smile was teasing. "And by passion, I mean your fiery temper."

"I'm tempted to mention your cold indifference," she said smoothly, "but I promised myself, and my sisters, that I wouldn't be rude to you tonight."

"Then you've succeeded. Almost."

His dry tone and barely hidden grin teased a laugh out of her.

"See that, Sami? We can get along. Before you know it, we might actually trust each other."

"Let's not push it," she muttered.

"How about this for now? I believe you only want to protect innocent lives. All I ask is that you believe the same of me. Can you do that?"

Since his commitment to that very cause was apparent, she said, "I can do that."

He shifted and held his hand out. "Truce?"

She took a moment, staring at his offered hand as if it might strike like a snake. Then she angled her arm across her body to grasp his hand in hers. "Truce." But his strong hand felt entirely too hot against hers.

She tried to pull away.

He held on. "So now will you tell me whatever it is you've been holding back?"

Her head filled with panic, half because of his burning touch, and the other half because of his probing question. She slipped free, her elbow bumping the table as she did. She glanced around, but the others continued to banter.

Picking up the dessert menu the server had left after clearing plates, she focused on the description of the German chocolate cake instead of Grayson. *How can he possibly know I'm hiding something?*

They'd just called their own truce. They'd shaken hands over it. But Sami still couldn't bring herself to tell him about the ring.

"Whatever it is," he said, refusing to let the subject lie, "I'm guessing you're keeping it secret for an emotional reason, a personal one. I just can't figure out what or why."

Sami kept her head down. "Don't know what you're talking about." But she did. The shame and guilt rose up to taunt her, and her throat tightened at the idea of telling him what she'd done. How she'd brought the monsters here with her careless actions.

"You can't let your emotions rule you, Sami. They won't serve you in battle. They'll only betray you. Logic, strategy, preparedness. These are the things you can rely on."

When she didn't reply, he cursed softly. "Why can't you just be honest? What do I have to do to prove we're on the same side?"

The whiff of temper sparked her own. "Fine, I'll be honest." She tossed down the menu.

"Great." He faced her fully, propping one arm on the table.

"Your secret society exists to fight Iele. To wipe vampires off the face of the earth." She spoke quickly, trying to get it all out before she could think better of revealing her true concern.

"That's been established," he said. "And?"

"So if supernatural beings are a threat, then what's your plan for humans who have power?"

"What?" He sat straight, shock and insult rolling over his face.

"Yeah, LeRoux. That's what I'm asking." Now she didn't look away. She held his eyes with her own. "I want to know if you also hunt witches."

# 12

Inside, Grayson hardened. "Well, you've broken your promise, Sami. Because that is truly offensive."

But even as the insult stung, he couldn't help but follow her logic. "I know people haven't always been kind to witches—biased trials, torture, pressing by stone, and burning at the stake." He drew a deep breath. "So I'm going to try and understand where you're coming from and, if I can, put your mind at ease."

He could see the indignation she'd worked up begin to melt away. Her shoulders dropped slightly, and she unclenched the fist in her lap. "Okay," she said. "I'm listening."

"First of all, our secret society, as you call it, exists to take care of one thing, and only one thing. *Iele.* When humans are bitten, even though they were innocent victims, they are physically changed. Their blood becomes Iele, and so do they."

"I get that," she said, "I really do. They then become a danger to others."

"Exactly." Grayson recognized the acceptance in her expression, her willingness to listen. "Sami, you and your sisters are not in the same category. Not even close." He picked up his beer only to find it empty, then set it back down. "I've encountered people with power before, though nothing like what the three of you have."

"Mom, Brit, and Granddad, too."

Grayson held still a moment, studying the tense lines around her eyes, and finally grasped the full picture. Had she actually been afraid he would wipe out her whole family? "I'm sorry you believed we might hurt you and those you love." So much about her behavior crystallized, her reason for distrust becoming clear.

"Look, Sami. It's true you and I don't know much about each other, besides the fact we have a shared enemy, but we have to decide if that's going to be enough." He took a long, heavy pause. "Because we may not have much time."

Now she gave him laser-like focus. "What do you mean? Time until what?"

"I don't know, and that's what scares me the most." The uncertainty, the fear of a full-fledged Iele invasion, chilled him to the marrow of his bones. "Sami, I've been fighting Iele for a long time, but I've never seen so much activity in one town. And the originals coming here. After centuries of staying away?"

"Part of that is because of us and the Jeweled Ceffyl. We told you that."

"Maybe, but something's got them stirred up, something happening on the other side. You said yourself you'd never encountered any before last year."

She nodded, unable to deny the rationale.

"I think bigger trouble is coming," Grayson said, before following up on the question that always seemed to surface. "This artifact Malrik thinks you can help him locate, was it the horse? The Ceffyl? Is he sending his men to search for something they'll never find?"

Sami averted her gaze, worrying her bottom lip. "Grayson, I think I should—"

"Hey, guys," Finley interrupted, stretching his arm forward and rapping his knuckles on the table.

As one, Sami and Grayson turned their heads, and he couldn't stop the huff of air from escaping. Every time he tried to get an answer . . .

"Let's settle up," Finley said. "Fiona's made us an offer we can't refuse. Buffaloberry pie." He wiggled his brows. "She says two are ready and waiting at her shop. They just need to be popped in the oven. So we voted to move the party over there."

Grayson didn't know what a buffaloberry was, and that was just one more answer he wouldn't be getting yet. Everyone started shuffling, preparing to go while Jack and Finley argued over who would get the check.

Letting his friend handle the bill, Grayson allowed his frustration to dissipate, deciding he'd revisit the artifact before the night was over. "I guess we should include the others in this conversation anyway," he told Sami, rising as she did.

She gave him a curt nod before they eased away from the table and headed for the parking lot on the side of the hotel grounds. While they'd enjoyed their meal, the moon had replaced sunset, casting a pale-yellow sheen over the gardens.

"It's such a nice night, and the store isn't far," Fiona said, looking back over her shoulder to Sami and Grayson. "Why don't we walk?"

"Sounds good to me," Grayson replied. The summer evening was perfect, and traveling on foot gave him a better opportunity to get a feel for what was out there. To pick up on any sounds or smells that shouldn't be there.

Any danger lurking in the dark.

Sami fell into a natural stride beside him, and her light scent drifted to him. Floral, but not heavy or cloying. Natural, as if she'd rubbed wildflowers on her skin.

The intimacy of that thought had him clearing his throat and lifting his face to the breeze. He needed to clear that image out of his mind.

Because imagining Sami's skin was a distraction he didn't need, one he couldn't afford.

"LeRoux," she said suddenly, and the erotic picture burst like a fragile bubble.

"I want to share something with you," she told him, "in the spirit of our new truce."

Grayson played it cool, hiding his expectation that she would bring up the artifact. If there was one thing he'd learned about Sami Whiteburn, it was that she didn't respond well to being pushed.

"I've got a spell in mind, one that could help us protect Bar Harbor."

"Mmm," he murmured, hoping she didn't pick up on his disappointment.

"I've been spending some time with my family's Grimoire. It's ancient and has information about the Fae that goes back hundreds of years. The different species, their weaknesses, their history."

Stunned, he gripped her upper arm. "You have this available *now*?"

"Yeah," she said, apparently unaffected by the light hold he had on her.

Still, he released her.

"I had no intention of telling you about it, but I will," she assured him.

"Thank you. I won't ask if I can send the book to headquarters for analysis, but I hope you'll let me make notes on what I think is important."

"I'll have to clear it with the family," she said, "but I'm sure they'll agree." She loosed a long sigh. "What you said at dinner makes sense. We do have a common enemy, and to be honest," she glanced his way, "I don't feel threatened by you. Not really. I just couldn't ignore the possibility of you targeting all things supernatural."

"Including witches who can conjure fire from nothing but the power of their blood."

"Now you're just trying to sweet-talk me," she teased, her steps keeping a steady tread on the sidewalk. Trees overhead blocked the light, so he couldn't see the emotions playing across her face. Yet he heard laughter in her voice.

"Anyway," she continued, "I've been studying the grimoire and have a protection spell worked up, but it only covers a certain range. I think I can protect most of the town, at least the most populated area, but I'm missing a crucial element."

"What element?" Grayson asked.

"Oh," Sami hedged, "just a little blood from an original."

"An original Iele," he said, though clarification wasn't really needed. Unsure what to add—and bombarded by notions of toad's toes and eye of newt—he walked on in silence.

"Why do you sound skeptical?" she asked at length.

"I'm not saying anything."

"Yeah, but your silence is loaded with disbelief."

Careful here, he told himself, worried about ripping apart their new and very fragile treaty. "I've seen what you and your sisters can do, so I'm not doubting your ability. I just have a hard time putting my faith in things I can't see."

When she didn't reply at once, he worried he'd pissed her off, that he'd shaken the small amount of trust they'd built.

"I get that," she said, surprising him. "By your own description, you're a man of logic. You rely on the familiar, the tested, and things you can control. That's what keeps you and others alive."

Her words, her appreciation for who he was, meant more to Grayson than he'd known it would. With renewed hope for a strong alliance, he was about to compliment Sami on her diplomatic delivery when Fiona spoke from the front of the group.

"Let's take this route," she said. "This street ends right next to the shop."

They crossed over the main road, and instead of taking Cottage Way, a street Grayson knew, they continued on for another block, making a right turn that took them to a road lined by looming trees. Soon they passed a large house with metal sculptures glinting in the vast moonlit yard.

"That's a nice place," Sami told him. "A bed and breakfast. Where are you guys staying?"

"Somewhere a little less . . . well, a little less. We'd stick out in a place like that."

Sami chuckled, the sound pleasant and warm. "Yeah. The three of you don't exactly scream tourist."

Beneath her words, Grayson heard what sounded like another voice. He stopped abruptly. "Did you hear something?"

"No." Sami spoke low. "But I don't have your enhanced senses."

Cocking his head and holding still, Grayson listened.

Finley and Dodge halted in their tracks as well, with Dodge holding up a hand to quiet the others.

"Fiona!"

Standing in a shaft of moonlight, Sami smiled. "But I heard that," she said, just as Fiona let out a happy laugh and raced ahead.

A man jogged out from the shadows and swept her up into his arms. Judging by the kiss they shared, Grayson assumed they knew each other. "Would that be Ronan, the Legion soldier?"

"The one and only." Sami's features softened with affection. "He's home. He's finally home."

Grayson heard Ronan tell Fiona, "Your mother told me where you'd gone for dinner. I decided to park at the shop and come to meet you."

"I'm so happy to see you." Fiona tightened the hug again.

The lovers then broke apart, somewhat reluctantly, and rejoined the group. Fiona held Ronan's hand, radiant with joy as she brought him over to greet the others.

She was still beaming when the wind shifted.

And Grayson caught a scent.

"Finley. Dodge." The way he said their names was all his men needed. Without a word, they spread out, instinctively taking up positions to protect the civilians.

"Where?" Sami asked, scanning the dim area, her palms glowing white.

And while her magick rose to meet the threat, Grayson palmed his weapon. Together they stood ready.

As vampires emerged from the dark.

# 13

Three hulking fiends strode casually, as if they had no fear of the humans who all stood ready to fight.

Tate pulled something from her purse and tossed it to Jack. Then she quickly dropped the bag and called fire to her hands, as both Sami and Fiona had already done.

Ronan held a curved blade he'd had concealed in his clothing, so with Grayson, Finley, and Dodge, they were eight—all armed and with a history of putting Iele down like rabid beasts.

And yet, the vampires approached. No battle posture. No darting glances. No bared fangs.

An ominous sense of dread coiled inside Grayson's gut. How had they gotten so close without his detection? Why did they act so differently from all the Iele he'd faced before, even the originals at the Whiteburn house?

As the creatures slowly advanced, that coil of dread reared up and struck hard.

"You smell of the land called Faerie," one of the brutes said, murder-red eyes on Ronan. "I'll feed on you first."

Ronan didn't respond.

"You can save yourselves from pain like you've never encountered," another of the vampires said, his chiseled features full of menace, "and give us the ring. Do so, and we will be merciful. Your deaths will be swift."

*Ring?* The single word hit Grayson like a sledgehammer, and he sucked in a sharp breath. The missing link.

Sami's secret.

But he let the revelation slide away. He couldn't break his concentration.

Something in the way these vampires moved—subtly and with fluid grace—told of a strength restrained. The three had surely been sent by King Malrik, and terrible suspicion had Grayson tightening his grip on his weapon.

Malrik had tired of losing his scouts in the human world, so this time, he'd sent true soldiers. Warriors.

His fighting elite.

"Be ready," Grayson told the others.

"They're different," Sami whispered beside him, alarm a slick undercurrent in her tone.

Grayson felt the same apprehension crawling down his back. "I know." He edged forward. "You should fall back."

"Screw that, LeRoux." Her words rasped with fury.

"Where is it?" Taking charge, the fiend who'd asked for the ring stepped forward, with the slightest ripple of aggression in his body language.

*He's preparing to attack.* Years of combat had honed Grayson's instincts, and though understated, the vampire had telegraphed his next move.

No one spoke. No one gave any indication they'd even heard the demand for the ring, and the standoff continued.

Until Grayson caught a flicker in the vampire's bloody gaze. He jumped to intercept, wielding his dagger when the monster sprang toward Fiona.

Slicing upward as he leapt, Grayson aimed for the bastard's heart. But he missed entirely, the vampire becoming a blur as he sped from harm's way.

Ronan's intended strike went off course as well, and Fiona's flash of white flame hurtled uselessly through the air.

"Fuck me," Dodge uttered. "They're fast." He whirled to face the second vampire, the one in a tight black T-shirt who'd lusted for a drink of Ronan.

Mimicking the same pattern as Grayson and his men, the three Iele spread out. But they circled the humans, their intent to attack rather than defend.

Grayson chanced a look to Sami, then cursed himself for taking his eyes of his foe. *She can take care of herself.* As he primed for a brutal fight, he prayed that was true.

"Ten." Grayson growled the order, telling his men to center their assault on the enemy in the ten o-clock position.

"Ronan, Jack. Your right flank," he said, hoping the men would cooperate. And finally, "Ladies, you have my back."

Then everything happened at once, an explosion of activity with a string of lightning-fast moves in a domino effect. Grayson launched his dirk toward the ten o'clock vamp as Dodge and Finley closed in at the same time.

The airborne dagger surprised the fiend, and the blade sank deep, piercing the black T-shirt and his chest to inject a surge of gold. Dodge and Finley landed on the vampire as he roared, his ability to fight back already slowed by the effect of poison in his blood.

Grunts and snarls erupted from behind, and as soon as the downed monster began to shrivel and die, Grayson spun around, ready to enter the fray. He pulled a second blade, filled with another shot of gold.

The glimmer of hope he'd felt from the first easy kill died when he saw the speed and agility of the remaining two Iele. They dodged and evaded, shifting from place to place faster than the human eye could track.

"Damn it!" Sami's shot went wide as she pursued the leader. Clearly the best of them, he stopped to materialize—teasing, taunting—before disappearing to avoid the lethal white fire.

Only he didn't actually vanish into thin air. He was simply that fast.

The third fiend, who'd so far been silent, also slipped in and out of range. Only he and the leader remained, but they didn't stay in place long enough for Grayson to command a direction.

For a few terrifying moments, the vampires zipped back and forth, giving Grayson the sense that he and the others were nothing but mice. Mice being toyed with by two vicious cats.

He was waiting for one of them to pounce, when a horrific sound—part-hiss and part howl—echoed through the night. Ronan had caught the silent one under his arm, slowing the vamp down enough for Jack to land a blow with his axe.

Grayson, Dodge, and Finley all made moves toward the injured Iele, going in for the kill.

When three bursts of ivory flame ensnared the beast. He fell to the street, writhing in agony, while Sami and her sisters stood by, watching to ensure his death.

*One more to go.* Regulating his breathing, Grayson let his keen eyesight do its work. The remaining vampire, the final threat, zipped up into a tree, a shaking limb and quivering leaves the only sign of his departure.

"Quiet." Holding up a hand, Grayson listened for the slightest rustle, the tiniest scrape, doing his best to track the creature as he moved through the branches, vaulting from tree to tree. *The bastard is good. Stealthy.*

And he could drop down on them at any time.

Without needing to say a word to each other, Sami, her sisters, and the other men closed ranks, backing up to each other in the middle of the street. Eyes on the towering maples and oaks, they maintained the quiet. So Grayson could listen.

Somewhere above a deafening *crack!* resounded, followed by a loud thud combined with a metallic clang off to the side.

As one, they all turned their attention to the yard of the bed and breakfast. Despite the low light, Grayson could make out a long, thick limb lying on the ground beside one of the sculptures.

A broken limb. That's what they'd heard in the trees. Then the creature had thrown the branch to hit the sculpture. To make a noise.

To create a distraction.

With sickening clarity, Grayson understood the vampire's ploy. He spun around, started to shout a warning to the others. But he was too late.

Dodge emitted a scream of rage, throwing punches over his shoulder to the devil on his back. The vampire had dropped and grabbed him from behind, and with preternatural strength, was crushing Dodge in his arms.

Then he lifted his head high, jaws wide and fangs bared.

"No!" Grayson yelled, rushing to help his friend as the monster leapt backward, hauling Dodge up, away, and into the dark.

Grayson raced after them, following Dodge's curses and shouts with the others on his heels.

An empty parking lot sat beyond the line of trees, where two figures grappled on the ground. Suddenly, the vampire bellowed, scrambling across the pavement like a spider.

Dodge's blade must have finally struck home.

As they all raced to Dodge, Grayson was grateful for whichever one of the sisters torched the Iele. He'd gladly let them finish him off.

While he took care of his friend.

"Dodge." Grayson dropped to the ground beside the man who'd fought beside him for half of his life. The friend who'd saved his ass more than once. The brother he'd laughed with, mourned with, and loved like family.

Finley appeared and gripped Dodge's left arm. "Dodge, man. Tell me you're okay."

"He got me. I'm bit." Dodge's face contorted with pain. "Fuck. I can feel the burn. It's moving fast."

"Just hold on," Finley told him. "Damn it, hold on!"

Dodge groaned, gasped, and began to shake.

Denial tried to lodge in Grayson's chest, but a lifetime of training and preparation took over, replacing denial with determination. The moment he always feared had arrived, and he had no choice but to deal with it. Swiftly. Mercifully.

Dodge had been bitten by an original. He'd been *fed on*. And despite decades of research, there was no cure.

Dodge's eyes, full of miserable acceptance, went to Grayson and then to Finley. "Don't be sad now. We had a hell of a run."

Finley could only nod, taking Dodge's hand in his own.

Dodge slid his gaze to Grayson again, and they glinted with steely resolve. "You know what you've got to do."

"I know. Let me look first." Grayson tried to keep his voice even, but it almost broke. Almost. "Where?" he asked, knowing Dodge would understand. "My arm. High up. Maybe my shoulder."

Over Dodge's head, Grayson and Finley shared a glance. They both knew what that meant. A limb could be severed to stop the flow of poison, but the shoulder . . .

Out of the corner of his eyes, Grayson noted Jack and Ronan coming closer, while Sami and her sisters surrounded the dead Iele.

Using his blade, Grayson ripped Dodge's shirt. Crimson trails ran down his arm and chest from two swollen puncture wounds, their location medial to the shoulder joint, near the collar bone.

In horror and shock, Grayson watched as black lines began to streak from the wounds. *The venom*. Soon it would reach Dodge's heart.

"He was going for your subclavian." Grayson spoke matter-of-factly, though inside he raged with pain and loss. "Too far in."

Dodge closed his eyes and nodded. "Peace out," he said and grinned. "I love you guys."

A strangled sound came from Finley, as if he struggled to contain his grief.

Grayson thought he heard Jack call out to Tate, but he couldn't think past the roaring in his head. He had to close off all emotion and do what had to be done.

"You don't have to say it back." Dodge's breathing was coming faster. "Because I know. I know."

Grayson felt like his chest was being crushed as he lifted his dagger. And said the words. "I love you, too, brother."

He hovered the blade over Dodge's heart. He raised it up.

"Stop!" Sami on the other side of Dodge, her hand extended and fingers curled.

An invisible and immovable force held Grayson's arm in place. "Let me go, Sami. This has to be done."

"No, it doesn't." She used her power to fling his dagger away.

He heard it clink against the cement and gained his feet. "Stay out of this. You don't know—"

"I *do* know." She actually shoved him with both hands before falling to the ground beside Dodge. "Ronan?"

"I have them. Here." The brown-haired soldier poured small crystals from a tube into her hands.

"There's no time," Grayson said, clasping onto Sami's shoulder, ready to pull her back so he could save Dodge before he changed. Before he became a monster.

Sami whipped around, her liquid brown eyes full of urgency but calm. And confidence. "I know this goes against your training. I know you're fully prepared to do the hardest thing. But just wait."

"I can't." An aching black hole opened up in his chest. "We made a promise to each other."

"Let us work, and you won't have to keep it." Her face softened. "Trust me, LeRoux. It's time to have a little faith."

Looking down at Dodge again, she pressed her hand against the bite wounds, her palm filled with the small clear stones Ronan had given her.

Tate kneeled on Sami's left, Fiona on her right. They each put a hand on her.

Sami's voice rose up, silvery and light, as if the sound itself carried magick. "Blood is red. Black is dead."

The intonation poured from her lips. "The dark is wrong. It doesn't belong."

Grayson sensed a tremor, a quickening in the air.

"Give this poison back to me." Sami's pitch rose. Her intensity grew. "As I will, so shall it be."

Quickly, she started the chant again, with her sisters joining in, adding their voices, adding their power.

As they cast their enchantment a third time, a soft glow emanated from beneath Sami's hand, so faint Grayson wondered if he imagined the pale pink light. Like a mystical vapor, it wavered and spread, evaporating into rose-colored motes that danced on the air.

He held his breath, staring at Dodge's lax face. *He's gone. It didn't work.*

A hand fell to his shoulder and he turned his head. Finley. Grayson hadn't realized the other man had come to stand with him.

At last, the women stopped, and Sami pulled her hand away. She poured what looked like tiny rocks back into the tube Ronan held. They were a putrid black.

"Dodge," Fiona said, gently stroking his cheek. "Can you hear me?"

Tate tugged on Grayson's elbow, so he crouched down and took her place. "Dodge." He fought against the flare of hope flickering to life. No one came back from a bite like that. Especially not the bite of a pure-blood Iele.

That's what he told himself. That's what he knew to be fact.

And that's why his heart tripped when Dodge's lids fluttered open, and his eyes shone clear. No red to be found.

Blinking a few times, Dodge glanced around before landing on Grayson and Finley. "Why am I still here?"

Fiona patted his cheek. "Because we like you, and we weren't about to let you go."

"Witches," Dodge whispered with a smile. "Everybody should have one."

A harsh laugh burst from Grayson, and he felt Finley slapping him on the back saying, "I'll be damned. I'll be *damned*."

"He should be okay." Sami also touched Grayson on the back. "But you'll want to stay with him, watch him until the wounds start to close."

He could see for himself that the injuries were clean. No jagged black lines crawling over flesh, spreading to the heart. Aside from Dodge's own blood, his skin was clear. The poison was gone.

"We'll get him to the hotel and take care of him. Call in medical to be safe." His head spinning and his thoughts muddled, Grayson rubbed his palm over his face.

So much had happened tonight. So much had been revealed.

And beneath the relief, he remembered. His body went rigid as he told Sami, "I'll make sure Dodge gets the best of care. That he gets whatever he needs to recover." Still studying his friend, he said, "And then I'll be coming to see you."

Facing Sami, he held her wary gaze. "So you can tell me all about the ring."

# 14

Cloaked Ridge
The Ielonaar Realm

Malrik's vipera banked hard, flying up and over the mountaintop, where dense gray mists veiled the craggy peaks. Astride the huge serpent's back, he crested the highest point and then dove back down. Down to his target, the widest expanse of clear ground.

And the best place to land a squadron of dragons.

His own vipera arrived first, landing deftly on the rock-strewn landscape. Before dismounting, Malrik rubbed the broad black head and the jagged crimson streak for which the creature had been named. Fulgar. An ancient and revered word for lightning.

Soothed by soaring in the sky with his mighty Fulgar, Malrik patted the beast and stroked its neck. He earned a contented growl in return, the fearsome sound a balm to his rage, to the anger still sizzling in his brain.

Since the blind seer had escaped his grasp, fury had been a constant companion, a relentless reminder. A sharp thorn in his side.

His gauntlet creaked as his fingers clenched on Fulgar's reins. How had Hellana known he was coming? How had she spirited away herself, the oracle, and all those in or near Draviski Castle?

One of Malrik's captive wizards had sworn the oracle's visions had been blocked, that her powers had been bound for the three days prior to Malrik's invasion. Yet somehow, Hellana had learned of his imminent arrival.

Even now, that wizard's wife festered with wounds, gashes sustained from her forty lashes. Not her punishment, but her husband's. For Malrik *would not* abide failure.

Rage burning anew, Malrik relished the brisk wind with its clean scent of ice and snow. Two of the only things present in these barren heights—ice, snow. And stone.

Yet over these rugged and lifeless lands, Malrik ruled with a bloody fist. As he ruled over those who served, those who followed, and those who resisted.

A screech announced the arrival of the vipera squadron—along with his prize—and a cruel smile pulled at Malrik's lips. *They don't resist for long.*

Most kingdoms of the realm had felt the bite of his blade, and those who remained secure did so only with his pardon.

Though iron-hued vapors hung low on the mountains, an even darker cloud gathered now. A swift and churning threat, a merciless storm, with beating wings like the sound of thunder.

One hundred of Malrik's fiercest warriors guided their vipera to the uneven ground. Two of the great serpents carried a wooden cage between them, and inside the enclosure rode Malrik's special guests.

His savage mood took a lighter turn as one by one the dragons landed. Each brutish animal boasted their king's colors, bred over centuries to be crimson and black. Their banners warned of Malrik's arrival, a heralding of death from the sky.

Once the serpents landed, the cage thudded over the scattered rocks. One of Malrik's men opened the door, dragging an old woman and a young girl from inside. The woman—the hag, as he thought of her—trudged toward Malrik, silent and stoic as ever.

The girl, though, quivered in the cold, her long golden hair slashing at her face in the ruthless wind.

Trying to position herself between Malrik and the girl, the white-haired woman came to a stop before him. Standing boldly, she glared into his eyes. "And so I am here."

As if in answer, rocks clattered down the steep ridge above. The loud noise startled a small cry from the girl. Malrik's men only laughed.

Yes, here she was, Malrik thought. The Mystic, the most powerful magick worker in the realm. Succumbing to his demands.

"Let us be done with this," the Mystic said, her lip curled in a hateful snarl. "Let us be gone from this ghastly and unforgiving place."

"You brought us here," Malrik reminded her with a spread of hands. "This is the place of your choosing."

"Aye, but not of my own will, you rot-hearted cur." She spat on the ground near his feet.

Fulgar snarled, and a few of the soldiers stiffened, unaccustomed to anyone daring to disrespect their king.

"No, not of your will." Malrik's voice whipped more harshly than the freezing gusts. "But of mine." He jerked his hand toward the girl, a few steps behind the old hag. "Bring her."

"Malrik," the Mystic began, her tone thick with threat, but her eyes filled with fear.

Malrik stepped close to the girl, the Mystic's beloved granddaughter. He slipped a rough gauntlet under her small chin. "No power in this one. A pity." He tossed an evil sneer to the Mystic. "But she has other gifts, I'm sure."

"Leave her be." The Mystic raised her fists, bound together at the wrists. "She is but thirteen. She is only a child."

"Yes, her bloom has only just begun." Malrik stroked the girl's pink cheek, and she flinched. "Yet that is when the petals are most tender, so sweet and soft."

"Harm her in any way, and I'll never do what you ask of me." The Mystic's face twisted with loathing. "Beware, Malrik, my magick can help you." She inched closer. "But my wrath will *end* you."

Malrik chuckled, the sound filled more with scorn than humor. "Hold no worries, Mystic, as you and yours will come to no harm, as long as you fulfill my request."

"My people have already come to harm because of your bloodthirst."

"Ah, but not all of your people." Malrik laid his hand atop the girl's blonde head. "Not your most precious."

He edged away, turning his back on the Mystic. A snub. Yet his words rode the icy breeze. "Your granddaughter is pure. She is unspoiled."

He stared over his shoulder, gazing into the woman's old but sharp gray eyes. "And so she shall remain," he said, his tone menacing, "if you do as I command."

"We're here, aren't we? In this frozen hell?" She thrust both hands upward. "There, beyond the jutting boulder, you will find a cavern."

"How big?" he asked.

She cast her gaze around the desolate landscape. "Big enough."

"Show me." Malrik lifted his chin to the soldier behind the Mystic. The man took her by the arm and tugged her along as Malrik marched ahead, toward the massive boulder.

As he made the short climb, he lifted a finger to the squadron leader and called, "Make ready."

The man bowed his head in deference.

Once beyond the hulking stone, Malrik discovered the cavern entrance as promised. Wider than a vipera's wingspan and higher than the marble pillars of his castle's grand hall. Again, his mouth curved wickedly. *This will do well.*

The scrape of feet on rubble told Malrik the others had arrived. "This is the best place?" he asked, not bothering to look her in the eyes.

"The perfect place," the Mystic returned haughtily. "I do nothing by half measures."

"Good. Good." Turning to her, he clasped his hands behind his back. "Then you understand what will happen if you fail me. What your *precious* will suffer if you attempt any deceit."

The woman blew air from her nose and ground her jaws together. After a long silence, her posture slumped. "I do," she said, and for the first time, she seemed defeated.

Around the cave's gaping mouth, the heavy stone flashed and sparkled. "What is this shining mineral?" Malrik asked.

"Na'raqui ore. The vein runs throughout this network of caverns."

"And this ore, this mineral, is why you chose the location?"

"It is. My magick is the kind born only once in a millennium, but for what you ask—"

"Can you do it?" he demanded sharply, cutting her off as he stomped over and took the side of her face in a vise-like grip.

"Aye! I can do it." Both revulsion and fear now lived within her glare. "I can." She shook off his hand, the white flesh pinkened from his abuse.

"For your granddaughter's sake, I hope you are right." Casting a steely look to the ominous sky, Malrik added, "She has already been spirited away. Even now, she is traveling to a place you will never find."

He dropped his gaze to hers again. "So you realize, you have no choice."

"Let me begin," was all she replied.

"You need no witch's tricks?" he asked. "No crystals or potions?"

To this, she only huffed, walking closer to the black mouth of the cave.

As her gravelly voice began to rise, Malrik crossed his arms, a dark pleasure growing inside.

He could already hear the screams. He could taste the blood.

And this was only the beginning.

# 15

Sami held tight to the grinder as she worked, focused intently on the sparking piece of metal as she shaped the beginnings of her new creation. She wore protective glasses, a face shield, and safety ear muffs for the grating noise.

Yet she sensed Grayson the moment he walked in.

Stopping, she set aside the grinder and removed her gear. "LeRoux," she said, pulling off her thick work gloves. "I expected to hear from you sooner." Almost two days had passed since the night they'd fought the Iele. The night Dodge had been bitten.

And the night Grayson had found out about the ring.

Now, with the time leaning toward four in the afternoon, he simply strolled through the barn doors she'd flung wide to allow a breeze.

She'd bought the old place for a song a few years back, as rundown and neglected as the house that had come with it. Then she'd turned her artist's vision and her worker's hands toward rehabbing both into her version of Bohemian chic.

For some reason, she felt suddenly anxious, having Grayson in her private space. Especially with his expression as flat and lifeless as the metal she molded.

"I wanted to stay with Dodge," he said, the nuance of his voice as level as his features.

Fear rolled through her like a flame to kerosene. "Is he okay? Did he get worse?"

"No. In fact, the very opposite." Grayson pivoted slowly, taking in her work station, raw materials, and completed sculptures. "I stayed with him out of sheer fascination."

He completed the turn and ended up facing her. "His wounds healed exceptionally fast, and he swears he feels as good as new."

Still unable to read him, Sami rubbed her elbow self-consciously. "That's good." She waited a beat, then, "Isn't it?"

"Yeah." He sighed heavily. "It is good."

She knew what Grayson had come to say, but he was drawing it out, tormenting her. So she decided to confront the issue head on. "You're still pissed about the ring. That I didn't tell you."

He jerked a shoulder. "Pissed is a stronger word than I'd use. Disappointed maybe."

Sami only nodded, because really, what could she say? She felt a little silly, not to mention paranoid, now that she'd had time to think, and to take a long, hard look at her own behavior.

She could admit she'd gone a bit overboard, and she'd let her misgivings run too far. But her intentions had been pure. All she'd wanted was to take care of her family, to keep them safe.

Still, she'd been wrong about him, so very wrong, and her only recourse was to swallow crow and make amends. So as he stood in her workshop taking in the scene, she stiffened her spine, drew a deep breath, and prepped herself to tell him everything. To tell him about the ring.

"I don't blame you for being disappointed, or even angry." She rubbed the flats of her palms together as she spoke. "I just hope you'll hear me out and let me explain why I kept the ring a secret."

Crossing his arms, he took up a comfortable stance as if settling in for the duration. "Oh, I'll hear you out. It's what I've been waiting for."

When her wrists ached from the pressure, she pulled her hands apart and said, "You know how Fiona freed the horse, the Jeweled Ceffyl." At his nod, she continued. "After that, we found out about a child, a newborn baby, who was in trouble."

Trying not to leave anything out, she took him back to the night of Emuirdane's death. He'd already heard most of the story from Tate and Fiona, so she concentrated on the moments after they'd saved Hellana's baby.

When Malrik had been too busy drinking Emuirdane's blood to even notice she and her sisters were there.

"Emuirdane's severed hand landed in front of me, and I saw the green stone glinting. It flashed at me like a beacon, like a warning light I couldn't ignore." Letting herself go back, Sami pictured the horrific night and the gruesome sounds of murder.

She curled her hand against her stomach. "I didn't think so much as react. I knew how much power the gemstone held, and I couldn't leave it behind." She glanced up to find him watching her closely, and shame burned her throat. "But maybe I should have."

"Why do you say that?" he asked, still calm and impassive.

"How can you even ask that after what's happened? You came here because of a dead body. Because someone was *killed*."

When he gave a slight nod, she threw up her hands. What would it take to get a reaction? "You tracked Iele activity to this place, to this town, because the ring is here. Because I all but invited those monsters to follow me, to come after Emuirdane's magick stone."

She strode toward him. "Why aren't you angry? What about what happened to Dodge?"

"Risk is part of our job, Sami. He could have been bitten anywhere."

"But he wasn't. He was attacked here," she jabbed a finger toward the floor. "*Here*. He was bitten by an original, because I brought them."

His right eye ticked, the first sign he was feeling anything at all. "So you blame yourself."

"Of course I do." Sami shook her head, bewildered. "How could I not?"

"So that's why you didn't tell me," he said. "You felt like you were responsible for the death of the young man we found."

"Partly," she hedged. "Okay, yes. I was ashamed. At first, I didn't want to share anything with you or your corporation, society," she waved a hand, "or whatever you choose to call it. But then, even once I began to trust you, and I knew you needed to know . . ."

She trailed off, rubbing her hands over her face. "I already felt guilty. Now I can add being stupidly blind."

"I don't see why."

"For not seeing things more clearly, for not giving you a chance. Tate and Fiona did, right from the start. So did my mother." She scoffed at herself, "Hell, everyone did. But not me."

"You didn't know who I was or why I showed up in your yard, at night, on the heels of a couple of creatures who'd come to kill you."

Sami stared in shock. He was actually justifying her actions? She hugged her arms to her midsection, unsure how to proceed. She'd expected fury and blame, but instead he handed her empathy.

"My sisters knew. They were right." She gave him a weak smile. "But that's usually how it goes with us."

"What do you mean?"

"Tate and Fiona always seem to know what to do, how to behave. They always have. Even when we were kids. After my mother died, or we thought she had," Sami swallowed the lump forming in her throat, "Tate and Fiona just fell into their roles as if it all came naturally."

She pressed her lips together and shut herself down. "Why am I telling you this?" And why was he listening?

"I want to know." He eased a step closer. "Tell me."

"I don't have to. You've seen for yourself. Tate is the practical one and always has been. She made sure things ran smoothly, helping Granddad and Brit, as if she were an adult like them. And Fiona, she fell right into her role. She became the caretaker, always with an instinct to nurture, to take care of others."

Grayson kept his eyes on her. "And what did you do, Sami?"

His rapt attention made her stomach tighten. She'd swear he was using his heightened senses to look inside of her, down deep to her hidden truths. Yet still, she let those secrets spill. "I entertained with my caustic humor. What else?"

Her laugh carried self-derision as she moved to pick up a discarded steel rod. She turned it in her hands, gripping until her knuckles strained. "No matter how hard I try, I always fall short. Look at what's happening now, what happened to Dodge. Because of what I did."

She hadn't heard him move, but he was suddenly there, easing the rod from her hands. He tossed it aside with a clatter. "Stop that. Stop blaming yourself for things beyond your control."

She huffed. "That's what my sisters said." He stood so close, too close. So she backed up and said insistently, "Taking the ring was a mistake. A *major* fuckup."

"You don't know that," he started, but she spoke over him.

"Yes. It was. And I should have come clean and told you sooner. I'm sorry. I put my pride before doing what was right. I was more worried about proving myself and only caused more problems. If you'd known about the ring—"

"I wouldn't have done things any differently." Annoyance creased Grayson's brow as his words lashed out. "So you can take that off your list of things you pile on your shoulders."

"I'm just trying to explain," she said quickly, at a loss for what exactly was happening. *Now* he was upset?

"You're explaining, all right, and I think I finally understand. Yes, Tate is levelheaded, clearly a left-brainer. And Fiona, well, she's got a heart as big as Texas. But we all have our gifts, Sami, and from the little time that I've spent with you and your sisters, I don't believe they blame you for the Iele presence here. And neither do I."

Sami's mouth fell open, and she could do nothing but listen.

"I don't see where you've made a mistake. In fact, what I see is a woman who fights hard and stands up to any challenge, especially when it comes to taking care of those she loves."

"LeRoux," she whispered, feeling too exposed, too raw and vulnerable.

His gaze gentled, lost some of its burn. "As far as I can tell, your only downfall is that suspicious mind of yours. And your mile-wide stubborn streak."

"Takes one to know one," she said, but couldn't muster her usual sarcasm. Her safety net.

"But just look what else that mind can do." He waved a hand at her completed works. "You have an amazing gift, Sami. You have the ability to see what's not there, to take individual pieces of what others would call junk and put them together to create beauty. To create art."

"It's a job." Uncomfortable, she glanced up to the rafters. Anywhere but at him.

"Not only a job. You don't give yourself enough credit. Take this piece," he said, gaining her attention again as he indicated a swirl of blue and gray, individual lines spiraling from a wide, rounded base and up to a delicate point. "The shape reminds me of a flame, but the fluidity is like water, maybe wind."

He pointed a finger. "I'm guessing that's tin and maybe some iron. I can't imagine how you pulled out the iridescence or the time it took to get those paper thin points."

"You're talking about skill, LeRoux. Not personality."

"They spring from the same source." He looked swiftly back to her. "You can see the big picture, Sami, but only when you get out of your own way."

He surprised her then, advancing and taking her by the shoulders. His depthless gaze penetrated hers. "What would have happened if you left the ring that night?"

Having his hands on her caught her off guard, as did the

demanding question. "I . . . um. Malrik would have gotten it."

"So what?"

"So . . ." Sami stuttered to a halt. Did this need to be explained? "He would have possessed both of Emuirdane's stones, the brooch and the ring, and all of the magick they held."

"And that would have been bad."

"Of course it would have been bad. Who knows what he could do with all that power?"

"Exactly," Grayson said, a sly grin gradually spreading over his handsome lips. Releasing his hold, he drew back.

"Yeah. That would have been bad." Crossing her arms, Sami pursed her lips and narrowed her eyes. *Sneaky bastard.* "Okay," she said, with more than a little reluctance. "Point taken."

"Good. So the heart of the problem isn't the ring. It's Malrik," he clarified. "And the question is why does he need the ring's magick?"

Sami shrugged. "Rook says he's a power-hungry sadist who wants all of the Iele to bow before him. And," she said, feeling slimy for even having the thought, "maybe if I'd left the ring, Malrik would be their problem instead of ours."

"Maybe." Grayson glanced again at the sculpture, lost in his own thoughts. "But one thing holds true for power-hungry leaders."

"And that is?"

"They can never get enough." The certainty in his statement held an ominous finality. "Even if he used the combined magick of two stones to dominate his world, there's no guarantee he would stop there."

Sami's skin chilled. It crawled with dread. "You think he'd come here next." The stark realization took her breath. "And with the two stones, he could. Emuirdane had the power to travel, anytime, anywhere, even without a portal."

"Because he had both the ring and the brooch."

"Yes."

"Still wondering if you did the right thing?"

"Not nearly so much." She punched her fist into her other hand. "I just assumed he wanted to control the Iele. I never thought he might come here."

And might never have if Grayson hadn't hounded her. If he hadn't kept firing his questions at her.

"I already gave you an apology," she said, "and now I need to thank you." The guilt she'd carried for months began to lessen, to lighten. "You're the one who saw this clearly."

She blew out through her lips. "So much for the big picture."

But she could be grateful she saw it now. With light steps, and a lighter heart, she went to a nearby table. She picked up the heavy object wrapped in burlap and carried it to Grayson. "Here. This is for you."

Brow crinkled again, he took the offering and peeled back the fabric. In silence, he stared down at the gleaming dagger. Softly, he traced a hand over the veins of gold fused with steel. "You made this," he said, with a hint of awe. "You made this for me?"

"High carbon. Abrasion resistant. Consider it a peace offering." Sami bit her bottom lip. "'Cause I've been kind of an asshole."

His laughter was low and deep, appreciative. "But you also saved Dodge's life. For that, and the stubborn streak that made it happen, I am very grateful." He folded the rough material back around the dagger and gave her a warm smile. "I think we're square."

"I'm making another now." She hooked a thumb over her shoulder toward the table. "I want to give one to Dodge and Finley. And as many of your men, or women, who want one."

"That's generous of you." The quality of his voice deepened, yet flowed smooth as honey.

Something entered his stare, and Sami got the impression his mind was no longer on weapons. She licked the lip where she'd bitten. "Like I said, I have some making up to do."

She told herself to run, to get out of the danger zone, but then she caught the teasing scent of clean, woodsy male. Her body betrayed her better judgment, and she leaned in.

The urge to wrap her arms around him and breathe him in was so strong, so consuming.

When she felt herself raise up to her toes, reality slapped her in the face. She jerked back, unsettled by the surge of attraction. Scowling, she snapped, "Damn it, what are you wearing?"

He notched his head back, clearly puzzled by her outburst. "What?"

She waved agitated fingers in his direction. "Your cologne."

"I don't wear cologne."

"Then what the hell is it?" She could hear how crazy she sounded but couldn't stop.

He managed to look both offended and bewildered. "I don't know. Soap?"

"Then don't."

Now he angled his head and hiked a brow. "Don't use soap?"

"Come on, LeRoux." She gritted her teeth. "You know exactly what I'm talking about."

His back went rigid, arms stiff at his sides. "I really don't."

But she could see he did.

"Oh, no?" She moved fast, crowding him, and was darkly satisfied by his sharp intake of breath. Brushing her thumb over his bottom lip, she whispered, "Now who's lying?"

# 16

Wildfire erupted beneath Sami's gentle touch. Grayson's blood heated, pumped in his veins, and raced down south. "Don't," he said, even as his hands shot out to grip her waist.

*She shouldn't. I shouldn't.* Fractured thoughts flashed in his head but wouldn't connect to make sense. All he knew, and all that mattered, was the sweet sensation of her warm skin—on his mouth, under his palms.

"Sami," he said, her name half plea, half prayer. Still gripping her waist, just above the luscious flare of her hips, Grayson inched her closer. When she took her finger from his lips, he angled down, intent on taking her mouth. Taking, touching, tasting.

But then she froze, her body tightening under his hands. Her brown eyes, so dark with temptation, fluttered and widened. "I'm sorry." She ripped free, holding one hand to her heart and the other out to him. "I'm so sorry. I don't know what I was thinking."

"It's fine." His voice was a hoarse croak, so he cleared his throat. "Don't apologize. I just didn't expect—"

"I know. Totally my fault." Her cheeks pinkened, and the rosy hue only ramped up his desire to kiss her. "I'm just churned up," she said.

"We both are." Being cautious, he shoved his hands in his pockets before he could grab her again. And while he might be able to keep his hands off of her, his eyes simply drank her in. The tumbling curls, that fiery brown he couldn't quite name. The gypsy-brown eyes he could get lost in.

And now, after a brief connection with her body, he knew exactly how good she felt. Could easily imagine fitting himself against her long, lean curves.

His rampant imagination stoked the fires of lust all over again, and the aching need—the *yearning*—he had for her threatened to be his undoing.

"I can't allow this," he blurted, torn between walking away to save his sanity, or lowering her to the barn floor to soothe the ache.

Sami called to a part of him he didn't recognize, and the stranger in him imagined the things they could do together. The things they could do to each other. The surging strength of his own desire gave him a jolt.

In a rough, thick voice, he said, "This is a problem." One he'd seen coming and had carelessly ignored.

"What's a problem? Me?" She folded her arms and lifted one shoulder. Her pretty lips puckered slightly, as if she didn't know what to say. "I said I was sorry. I'm just emotional. After everything we talked about . . ." Another shoulder lift as she fell quiet.

"Emotional," he echoed, the very word pushing a hot button for him. "The one thing we can't allow ourselves to be. Not now."

"I agree." She gave a sharp nod, but her gaze had turned distant, dark eyes staring over his shoulder.

"Emotions are dangerous, Sami. They get people killed." He knew this to be true, from firsthand experience. The worst experience of his life, and one that haunted him still.

He never spoke of that night, not with anyone. But for reasons he was afraid to acknowledge, he wanted Sami to know. He wanted her to *know him.*

"I shouldn't have come on to you like that. I shouldn't have touched you." Still gazing away, she spoke stiffly.

"Don't apologize again. I wanted it," he admitted. He couldn't stand the hurt reflected in her eyes, or knowing he'd put it there.

"Sami, I want *you*."

She bit her lip, and her hand shook as she brushed at her hair. A stray lock had escaped from whatever was holding it back.

"But we have to stay focused." He had every intention of explaining, of telling her why he had to hold himself back. Why the feelings growing between them could be treacherous.

But instead, he reached out, unable to stop himself from stroking his thumb and finger down the silky, curling strand.

As if burned, he jerked his hand back, recognizing his own weakness. *I have to shut this down.* Her effect on him was just too overpowering.

"I'll make you a deal." Grinning, he tried for a joke to lighten the mood. "I'll stop using soap if you stop rolling in wildflowers."

"Wildflowers?" Her eyes shot to his, and a tiny wrinkle formed between her arcing brows.

"You think you don't drive me crazy? That your scent doesn't reach right in and—" He broke off, unable to describe the gut-clenching need. Instead, he touched her as she had him, stroking his thumb over her bottom lip, so soft and full.

Sami closed her eyes and sighed. She shuddered.

*Just one kiss. Just one taste.* The justification whispered in the back of his mind as his fingers trailed down to the side of her neck, and he lowered his mouth to hers. At first, the kiss was soft and undemanding. Safe.

Then it all changed, and they came together for one staggering moment of wild heat. Her hands slid up into his hair as she pressed her body to his.

The pulse in her neck throbbed under his palm before he dropped it and reached around her. Fisting his hand into her shirt, he lifted the fabric and slid inside, to the curve of her lower back.

The brief touch of skin on skin shocked as it burned, like a brand. Static roared in his head, blocking out everything in the world but Sami. Sami Whiteburn, the witch who fit so perfectly against him. Who fit—as if she'd been made for him.

Lost now, unable to resist, Grayson lifted her up to her toes, taking the soft whimper from her mouth into his own. He cursed himself, certain there was no stopping now.

Until a crooning male voice burst out. Sami pulled away, releasing a long, slow breath as she stared at him. Only then did he recognize the sound of Maroon Five, the lead singer promising to stay only one more night.

"My ringtone," she muttered, touching her lips in wonder as she backed up. "I should get it."

"Of course." Stunned by the strength—the shattering force of a single kiss—Grayson watched mutely as she returned to her work table and answered the phone.

*What am I doing?* He lowered his head and rubbed his temple. *What the hell am I doing?* After his lecture about emotions and staying focused, he'd lost complete control of himself.

Because Sami had a way of doing that to him.

He'd recognized the chemistry between them. Denied it, but recognized. He'd come here on a job, to keep people safe. And as far as he was concerned, that included Sami and her family, no matter how much magick they wielded.

But he couldn't concentrate on the mission when lust clouded his judgment. He couldn't see to anyone else's needs if he selfishly put his first.

Regret sat on his shoulders, like twin devils laughing at their success. But he shrugged them off in an instant when he heard the distress in Sami's voice.

"I'm on my way," she said, stuffing the phone in her back pocket.

"What's wrong?" Grayson asked, putting his personal worries aside.

"That was my mother. She said I need to come home." With only the briefest hesitation, Sami said, "You should come with me." Fear flitted over her face. "Kat got a message from Rook."

# 17

In less than ten minutes, Grayson pulled into the drive of the sprawling white Victorian.

"Looks like everyone's here," Sami said, surveying the other cars with her hand on the door handle. As soon as he parked, she jumped out.

Grayson kept pace with her long stride as she led him to a door on the side of the house. Once there, he stepped in behind her, to be met by the entirety of the Whiteburn clan.

Kat and Fiona sat at one end of a long wooden table with Sami's grandfather and Jack at the other. Behind them, a hearth of ivory brick framed a fireplace. Candles sat in a pretty display, replacing flames during the warm summer days.

Sami's mother, Nadia, offered him a welcoming smile as she flicked the button on the coffee maker. "Oh, Grayson. It's good you're here." If she wondered, or worried, why he accompanied Sami, it didn't show.

Then again, more critical issues likely occupied her mind, as well as those of everyone gathered here.

Grayson exchanged a nod with Ronan and Brit, the two men standing off to the side near a doorway, just as Sami's grandfather stood quickly and said, "There he is."

With surprising dexterity, the older man bounded to Grayson. He grabbed his hand and pumped. "I wanted to thank you," he said. "The girls told me about the other night. How things could have gone differently if you and your men hadn't been there to add your weapons to the fight."

"No need to thank me, Mr. Whiteburn." Humility tickled in Grayson's throat. Rarely did anyone know what he and his colleagues did on a regular basis, much less thank them for it. The appreciation was new, and oddly gratifying.

"I don't think I have to tell you that your granddaughters held their own," he told the older man. With a quick survey of the room, he added, "They all did."

"I'm sure they did, and it makes an old man proud. And you can call me Niall," he added before winking. "Once you kill a bloodsucking Iele, you're as good as family."

"Granddad," Sami said, sending a long-suffering look to the ceiling. Instead of sitting, she stood with her hands on her hips. "Okay, fill us in."

"Tate's just gone to—Oh, here she is." Sami's mother notched her chin up when Tate came in from a hallway.

"Sorry. Sorry." Tate held up her hands and plopped into a chair beside Jack.

"Right," Kat said, aware she would be the one to deliver the update. "Brit and Nadia already know, but I waited for all of you to get here before telling it again." Putting a hand to her stomach, as pregnant mothers were wont to do, she began. "Since my last experience with the bath, when I sensed Rook's fear, I've been . . . trying to keep the lines of communication open."

"She keeps a black bowl filled with water in the bedroom," Brit explained, putting a hand on his wife's shoulder. "And spends too much time staring into it if you ask me."

"I have to do something." Kat frowned. "So much is happening, and I need to help. I want to contribute."

"You *are* helping," Brit told her. "You're the only link we have to Rook's world and the only way we can get any information about what's happening there. And you're creating a life, which sometimes leaves you tired. So cut yourself a small break."

Kat sent him a thankful grin and slid her hand up to cover his. "I know. Still . . ." With a heavy sigh, she continued. "I was right to keep looking, because Rook contacted me today. He wanted me to pass on a message."

Now she looked at Fiona, Tate, and finally, Sami. "He wants the three of you to come to the Ielonaar Realm."

"What?" Ronan burst out, the same time as the voices of the other men rumbled with concern.

Grayson schooled his features and held his own reaction in check. He'd grown accustomed to stories of Sami and her sisters traveling to places they called "farworlds," but Kat's announcement was the last thing he'd expected.

As various discussions blended around him, the entire experience took on a surreal quality. So he stayed quiet and waited to see how it played out.

"He didn't say why, not specifically," Kat said, apparently answering a question Tate had posed. The others fell silent when she spoke. "He just said you need to come. There's to be a meeting of some sort, an assembly of significant people. Or significant Fae, I guess."

Kat shook her head. "I'm using my own words, because I could only make out the message in broken shards. The gist is that the meeting is important, and he thinks you would want to be part of it."

"This can't be good," Ronan said, his gaze seeking Fiona's. His mouth pressed into a grim line.

"You're right." When Grayson spoke up, no one seemed to mind. No one treated him as if he didn't belong or shouldn't be involved. Even Sami watched him with interest, open to his opinion.

Quite a change since the day he'd come for tea in the parlor.

"Rook could want you there for a number of reasons," he said, "but the convening of an assembly," he gestured to Kat, "a meeting of important Iele, probably means trouble."

"Maybe they only want our help." Sami prowled the room, rubbing her chin. "If it has anything to do with Malrik, they might want to question us. Or even Hellana. We've had encounters with both, and either of them could be the reason the Iele are riled up."

"I don't see Hellana reverting to her old self." Fiona sat back in her chair, shaking her head. "All she cared about that night was her baby."

"Anything is possible." Sami's mother pulled out the pot and poured herself a cup of coffee. "I know motherhood can be life-changing, but don't take anything for granted."

Grayson recalled that Hellana had been the wife of Emuirdane, the vengeful Iele woman who'd held Sami's mother in a sleeping spell for two decades. He had to agree with her words of caution.

"The only way to know is to go there and find out for ourselves." Sami stopped pacing. "Even if Rook only wants our help, if he only wants our input, that still means trouble's brewing. We can't afford to sit here and hope the problems don't spill over onto us."

"Fine." Tate laid her hand on the table. "Let's say we do go. How do we get there? We don't have a magick stone from a goddess to take us. We don't have a portal."

"Oh, I forgot." Kat grimaced. "I won't claim pregnancy brain, but I'm tempted. He said to use the pool to Faerie."

Grayson wasn't the only one who stared at Kat as if snakes were curling up out of her hair.

"No, no, no." Tate laughed harshly and touched Jack's arm. "There's no reason to return to Faerie." She looked at her husband then. "And you are *definitely* not going back."

"Winter Queen fatal attraction." Brit made a painful face. "Listen to your wife, Jack. Stay home."

Everyone laughed then, and a dreamlike quality descended over Grayson. How could they all be so nonchalant?

Then he considered his own life and how he coped. How he and the guys could joke with blood splatter still staining their clothes.

Gallows humor. He could relate.

"Trust him." Kat snapped her fingers. "That's what I heard after Rook mentioned the pool. That you should trust him."

Tate let her head drop back and groaned. When the others fell into contemplative silence, Grayson got the feeling a decision was being made.

"I'll go," Sami said.

"Anything we do, we do together." Fiona rose and went to Ronan. With sadness covering her face, she slipped an arm around his waist. "You just got back, and now I have to leave."

"Not alone you don't." Ronan cupped her cheek. "I hope the invitation includes plus-ones, because you're not going without me."

"Don't even try, Tate," Jack said when his wife turned to him as if about to argue. "You know it's pointless."

"But . . . *Faerie.*" Tate curled both hands to her chest. "We barely got out the last time, especially you. The queen would have kept you for herself."

"But you outwitted her, and we *did* get out. We're all better prepared now and," he waved an arm to encompass the others, "more strength in numbers." He chucked her chin. "And I believe we can trust Rook."

"I do, too, so I'll go," Brit said. For which he received a resounding chorus of negative replies, most of them citing Kat and the baby as reasons he had to stay.

"Plus, we need you here," Fiona argued when he wouldn't comply. "We can't be sure Malrik isn't sending more of his thugs right this minute."

"I still should go," Brit insisted.

Grayson could see he was torn. As their uncle, he probably felt duty bound to protect Sami and her sisters, but now he also had a wife and a child on the way. How could he have any peace of mind if he left them here? Bar Harbor wasn't completely safe.

"I'll go." Grayson's announcement drew all eyes his way. "My men can keep guard here. They can coordinate with Brit and the rest of your family," he said, throwing in a reason for Sami's uncle to remain home.

"You'd agree to travel to a farworld?" Brit asked. "Just like that?"

"I think I have to. There's no better way to get a handle on what's really going on over there." He waited for objections, but none came. They all seemed to be processing his offer.

As they did, he performed his own internal analysis, weighing the potential benefits against the risk. And concluded this was a one-shot chance, an opportunity that didn't come along every day. Or every century.

Sami edged closer and lightly touched his arm. "Are you serious?"

"You should know me well enough by now that you don't have to ask."

"No. I guess I don't." She dropped her hand. "But let's get one thing straight. You can't go into this looking for a fight."

"I won't."

"You understand why I have to say that."

"Sure." He'd made his aversion for Iele, for any Iele, clear from the start. "Maybe my misgivings are why you'd want me to be there. Balance," he said when she only blinked. "You've all decided Rook and this assembly of Fae are trustworthy, but I can't think that way. I have to assume they'll worry about themselves first. That they'll put their own world before ours."

"They'll protect themselves. Who wouldn't?" she asked, the arcs of brows clashing together. "But that doesn't mean they'll sacrifice the human world."

"Are you completely sure? Are all the Iele as honorable as Rook?"

"Hardly," she scoffed.

"Well then . . ."

"Okay. I get it. You still have to promise not to go in guns blazing." Her gaze fell to his belt and the sheath fastened there. "Or daggers either."

Grayson had to smile. "I'll go armed. But . . ."

"But?"

"I can admit when someone is more experienced in a certain area than I am. And when it comes to teleporting to Fae worlds, you and your sisters are the experts."

Now she was the one to grin. "Teleport sounds like we're in a futuristic sci-fi world, but I still appreciate your deference. And it's about time," she added with a smartass grin.

With a clap of her hands, she spun to face her family. "Okay. Grayson's in, unless anyone wants to vote him out."

Brit crossed his arms and didn't seem pleased, so Grayson took the opportunity to reassure him. "You'll be doing me a favor in return. I need you to keep my guys informed, assuming we're able to send you updates."

Kat stood and linked her arm with her husband's. When Brit's posture relaxed, Grayson knew he'd come to terms with staying behind. "I will," Brit said, extending his arm. "And thank you."

Grayson stepped forward and shook his hand. "No problem."

"Mom, I need your help." Sami crossed to where her mother stood by a bay window with a view of the front yard. "Can you finish the daggers for Dodge and Finley? I'd like for them—"

"Of course I can." Her mother set her mug on the sill and took Sami's cheeks between her palms. "It's a lovely gesture. You still have clothes here, or do you need to go home?" she asked, removing her hands.

"I can make do." Sami pivoted to Grayson. "We should go as soon as you can manage."

Pulling the phone from his back pocket, Grayson inclined his head. "I'll call Finley and let him know. My go-bag's in the car, and my guys will come pick up the vehicle soon."

"Don't worry about that," Sami's grandfather said. "Anything you need, just let us know." The older man patted Grayson's shoulder as he passed.

Grayson addressed Brit again. "You can work things out with Finley when he gets here. We've already called for another team. They arrive tonight."

After discussing the details with Brit, Grayson noticed Sami and her sisters had left the room, along with Ronan and Jack. Everyone packing for an unexpected trip.

To the realm of the Iele.

Grayson rolled his shoulders, wondering what he'd just agreed to, and then headed outside. On his way to the silver SUV, he called and relayed the situation to Finley.

First, he dropped the keys in the front seat, then he went to the back to grab his bag. Once he hung up with Finley, his eyes landed on the burlap bundle he'd set beside the duffel. Carefully, he unwrapped the dagger, the gift from Sami.

A place beneath his heart lurched. And he instantly scolded himself for getting sentimental over a weapon. As far as meaningful keepsakes, though, the finely-crafted blade was exactly his style.

He kept the concealed knives he already wore, rewrapping Sami's gift and sliding it inside his bag. And hoped he wouldn't need to use it on the other side.

"Ready?" Sami called, strolling across the grass toward him.

"As ever," he said, closing the cargo hatch.

She jostled the small backpack she carried. "This is the first time I've actually packed for a visit to a farworld. Makes me think these trips are becoming far too commonplace."

Without a clue how to answer, Grayson gestured to the house. "The others?"

"They're about ready. Saying their goodbyes." Her steps fell into a slow pace, keeping time with his as they strolled back. "I've already said mine, and it never gets easier."

"You worry," he said. "Not just about not coming back, but

about leaving them here alone."

"I guess you would understand that," she said and stopped to face him. "Dodge and Finley, they're good friends. They're like family."

Grayson felt another tug in his chest. Not only had he and Sami disbanded with the suspicion, they'd begun to find common ground. He wasn't sure whether to be grateful or wary.

His impenetrable logic couldn't keep taking these hits, or Sami would soon break down his walls.

He didn't have long to consider the breakdown, as Jack called their names from the side of the house.

"Speaking of family," Grayson said. But as he and Sami approached, he furrowed his brow. "Don't you all have obligations to deal with? Fiona, what about your store?"

"I've been training a part-time manager. She'll cover for me." Steely resolve sat in Fiona's green eyes. "I'd say this qualifies as a family emergency. Plus, time is different in farworlds. Days pass in the Ielonaar Realm, but may only be hours here."

"Tate and I are basically self-employed, and so is Sami." Jack glanced to Ronan. "And this one is in a life transition. From leading the army of a goddess to . . ."

"I'll let you know when I figure it out." Ronan raked a hand through his brown hair. "For now, I'm just happy to be here." He tugged at Fiona's arm. "But we'd better get going while the sun's still high."

Grayson fell in when they all started toward the back yard. As he passed the window above the kitchen sink, he raised a hand to Sami's mother who stood just inside. Brit was behind her, his arm around her shoulders, both of them wearing masks of unease.

Grayson met Brit's eyes. He inclined his head. And in that brief exchange, an oath was sworn.

They'd both stand and defend where the other could not.

Sun still shone for the long summer day, allowing glimpses

through the trees of the blue Atlantic beyond. But when Grayson trailed Sami into the forest, only thin shafts of light penetrated the thick leaves overhead.

With soft steps, their group pushed onward, moving without conversation until they broke free of the woods. Leading the way, Tate came to a halt beside a deadly precipice.

She had to raise her voice over the tide, crashing against jagged rocks fifty feet below. "The entrance to the tunnel is down there." She pointed as she explained to Grayson. "Steps descend across the face of the cliffs."

Then with a smile and a kiss for Jack, Tate began the climb down. One by one, the others followed.

"Careful of the wind," Sami said, before she too stepped off.

At the bottom, the stairway leveled out to a small platform, but Grayson couldn't see how they'd get past the wall of bedrock.

"Camouflage," Sami said, as if reading his mind. "We keep the opening concealed so curious wanderers won't be tempted to investigate." She watched as Tate said a few words and a cavern entrance appeared before saying, "These aren't your average underground tunnels."

Sami's tone had fallen flat, and a chill of foreboding crept down Grayson's spine.

Inside the black-as-night tunnel, the group paused. Sami and Fiona joined Tate at the front and, in sync, the three lifted their hands and recited a short chant. "Banish the dark and let us see. Show the way for the sisters three."

Rocks piled on the ground instantly lit up, the stacked pyramids emitting an eerie aqua glow at spaced intervals. "Impressive," was all Grayson could say.

Because the list of the sisters' remarkable feats never seemed to stop growing.

Again, they pressed onward, trekking through the winding shaft with stacked stones illuminating the way. The muted blue glow led them deeper into the earth and away from the last wisps of daylight.

Finally, the corridor narrowed and curved, sloping down before opening up to a vast cavern.

Fascinated, Grayson edged away from the pack and closer to the underground pool. Glimmering with unnatural light, a flashing waterfall ran from the rock above to feed the blue depths.

Points of light shimmered within the falling stream, sending wavering reflections of light to the stone walls and ceiling. And even more of the glowing rocks lay scattered on the bottom of the pond, lending their blue incandescence to the water.

Sami came to stand with him near the edge. "Mesmerizing, isn't it?"

"That's one word for it." Grayson studied the ethereal pool as other descriptions came to mind. Hypnotic. Incredible. Spellbinding.

Forbidding.

"The waters are poisonous," Sami told him, cementing his fears. "But they'll clear for us," she explained. "Tate was the one who started the quest for the Jewled Ceffyl after she found a mystical disc called a heolig." Sami nodded to the water. "The heolig went in there, and its power remains. All we have to do is repeat the words inscribed in the stone."

"With two little variations," Fiona said from Grayson's other side. He'd been so captivated by the blue glow and Sami's explanation, he hadn't noticed her approach. "The Ceffyl has now been released, so I think we should honor that."

"Why not?" Sami shrugged. "If it doesn't work, we'll just use the original."

With the decision made, Sami and Fiona lined up with Tate. They linked hands to form a unit, while Grayson stood with Jack and Ronan to observe from a distance.

"Trust the heolig from the heart. Poison waters to recede." Their voices danced in the air and echoed off the cavern walls. As one, they drew a breath and continued. "Daughters of Nadia found a way. The Jeweled Ceffyl has been freed."

Nothing happened.

"It didn't work, Fee." Sami leaned forward to look at her sister.

"All right. All right. Let's just do it the old way." Fiona huffed. "I mean, you'd think magick would know things had changed."

"It's what's written in the stone," Tate murmured, inhaling deeply for the second try. "Let's just follow the rules."

"Killjoy," Sami muttered, but the three of them only chuckled.

Again the trio of voices bounced through the cave, this time without pause. "Trust the heolig from the heart. Poison waters to recede. Daughters of Nadia find a way. The Jeweled Ceffyl will be freed."

A tremor rolled through the stony ground, and Grayson instinctively bent his knees for balance. The women eased back from the edge of the pond, though the quaking subsided almost as quickly as it had begun.

"Come see," Fiona said, waving to the men.

"I'm afraid I've seen it," Jack said. Still, he walked forward and, trusting their judgment, Grayson went along with him and Ronan. Together, they watched as ripples formed on the pond's surface.

"What's happening?" Grayson asked, amazed as the wrinkles in the pool grew to small waves. And awestruck when the pond split down the middle, the two sides building to great swells rising higher and higher against opposite sides of the now empty basin.

Sami's lids fluttered as a cool wind swept over them. "Magick," she said. "Magick is happening."

Bedrock lay on the bottom, but before Grayson could ask his next question, the stone shifted. It stirred. Darks tendrils arose from the rock, spreading and searching like fingers of black fog.

Soon other colors emerged in long, thick strokes. Pieces began to merge, to create a scene. A dense green forest, with the sounds—

and scents—of the tropics.

Grayson inhaled, stunned by the smell of lush vegetation and . . . ocean?

"That doesn't look like Faerie," Tate said, her relief obvious.

"Rook wants us in the Ielonaar Realm, so maybe . . ." Fiona let her supposition go unfinished.

Grayson's head pounded, but his chest felt light. "It looks so peaceful," he said. "So *normal*."

"Don't expect it to stay that way," Sami warned. "Wherever *that* is," she pointed, "it's a farworld. The dominion of the Fae."

She abruptly took his hand in hers. "LeRoux, I won't think less of you if you change your mind."

Oddly touched, he squeezed her fingers. "But I'd think less of myself."

With a firming of her lips, she gave one sharp nod. "I want to go first," she told him, her line of sight moving to the unearthly pool. She started to extract her hand from his.

"Don't," Grayson told her. "I'll go with you."

"Okay." She brought her liquid brown gaze back to his. "Then don't let go."

"I won't," he said, and for him the promise came from deep inside, from a place he'd never known existed. A foreign place where Sami now lived.

So, no, he wouldn't let go. He didn't want to let her slip away.

And that, he thought as together they leaped, was the thing that scared him most of all.

# 18

The sensation of falling stole Sami's breath. But in two quick beats of her heart, disorientation fled, and she stood in the midst of a lush green forest.

Just as they'd seen through the portal, the landscape gave off a tropical vibe, with exotic birdsong ringing through the trees and a lovely ocean breeze keeping humidity at bay.

Beautiful, she thought, and peaceful beyond belief. But upon closer inspection, all the beauty held an unfamiliar sheen, a barely-there glow of fantasy.

"This is not what I expected." Still holding her hand as promised, Grayson gripped her fingers once before letting go. "Like the Virgin Islands on steroids."

"There is that," Sami said as she examined a shrub with electric-red flowers wider than the span of her spread fingers. She reached out—and jerked back, remembering the enthralling blooms in Faerie. The ones that had drugged Tate with their sedative magick.

"Better not touch," she said to herself as much as Grayson. Sliding her eyes toward him, she studied his expression as he studied the alien surroundings, and had to give him credit for fearlessness. He'd jumped into the cavern portal with no hesitation, no second-guesses.

Only trust.

He'd literally taken a leap of faith. Faith in her and her family and their insistence that Rook wouldn't betray them.

She was still watching him when his eyes tensed the slightest bit, and she followed his stare to the Iele emerging from the fronds of two gigantic plants. "Right on time," Rook said, his mouth lifting in a half-grin and his blue eyes shining with warm welcome.

"Rook," Fiona said, rushing forward to give him a hug. "We came as soon as we could."

"But after a discussion about what could possibly have made you summon us." Tate, ever pragmatic, cut straight to the heart of the matter. Then she smiled. "But it's good to see you again."

"And you," Rook replied, meeting Tate and Sami halfway for a short embrace of them both. "Jack," he said, stepping away from the women to extend a hand. "And you must be Ronan." Another handshake before Rook turned his attention to Grayson. And stiffened.

"You are the tracker, then?" Rook demanded, all signs of amiability gone from his features. "The killer of Iele?"

"Uh." Sami edged closer to intercede. "If you picked up that much from Kat, then you can also sense he's an ally. A friend."

"I do, yes." Rook crossed his arms. "That's not all I'm picking up on," he added, his stare never wavering from Grayson.

"They told me you were perceptive," Grayson said. "So what vibes do you get from me?"

"Wariness. Cynicism." Rook angled his head and squinted. "But also a fair and sensible mind." His posture loosened. "Yet your first thought was to put a blade through my heart."

"You caught that, did you?" Grayson sent an apologetic look to Sami before telling Rook, "Honestly, it's habit. Training combined with instinct. You stepping out all of a sudden, with the vaguest trace of the monsters I kill tainting your scent." Grayson shrugged. "Call it a knee-jerk reaction."

This time, Grayson was the one to extend a hand. "My apologies. I can't promise the occasional murderous notion won't cross my mind, but I'll try to keep it down."

Rook's booming laughter surprised Sami into chuckling along with him. He heartily shook Grayson's hand. "Well, then. That's fair enough." He clucked his tongue. "Although, I don't like hearing I smell anything like Malrik's kind."

Grayson grinned. "Just barely."

"Good." Rook said, rubbing his palms together. "But with greetings out of the way, we should go." Gesturing for them to follow, he turned and tossed over his shoulder, "The council gathers soon. I'm sorry to give you such short notice."

"What's happening?" Tate asked. "Why are we here?"

Rook exited the jungle and stepped onto a paved trail winding along the edge of a sugar-white beach. His mouth flattened into a grim line. "There is much to discuss. If I can beg your patience for a little longer, all will be explained."

A bell tolled, drawing Sami's gaze to a sparkling city. Buildings of beige and ivory spread away from the shoreline, through a wide valley, and up the sides of verdant hills. Centered amongst it all and closest to the beach was an enormous palace.

Only slightly darker than the white sands, the stone edifice stood tall with domed towers rising to the sky. Masonry created lace-like patterns in various places and, along with tiled mosaics of blue and white, reminded Sami of ancient Persian architecture.

"The midday bell chimes. We are already late." Rook took off again, leaving Sami and the others no choice but to keep up.

He led them through gardens with hanging vines, some covered in flowers, past a large babbling fountain, and to a side entrance of the palace. The huge doors opened before them, two uniformed males inside holding the handles. "M'lord," one of them said to Rook with a bow of his head.

Sami shifted to Fiona and Tate. Their expressions of astonishment mirrored her own. Rook had never mentioned any royal ties.

Their footsteps echoed in the wide, tiled corridor, until Rook slowed and held fingers to his mouth. "The council has convened. We are expected, but . . ."

"We understand," Sami said. "But what about our weapons? They have gold," she added in explanation. The element was poisonous to Iele and could be considered an affront.

"As long as you don't pull one on any of the council members," he said cheekily and grinned, "you should be fine." Then he nodded at yet another pair of liveried doormen who allowed them entry.

Enormous columns lined a vestibule, guiding visitors to a chamber at the far end. Sami and the others made their way as calmly and quietly as possible, the smallest scuff of shoe on floor resounding through the great hall.

Though she shouldn't have worried. Voices masked their approach, some raised in heated debate as they filtered to Sami's ears. Still with no idea why she and her sisters were wanted here, the angry sounds raised hairs on her arms while anxiety curled in her stomach and made itself at home.

A raised and curving dais sat across the room. Four high-backed and ornamented chairs ranged along each side, seating a variety of male and female Iele. In the center and on a higher platform, a golden jewel-encrusted throne reigned above the others.

A man of noble appearance sat in the throne, his navy-blue hair and sculpted features similar to Rook's. Obviously the ruler here, he maintained calm silence as the other Iele disputed.

As Sami and the group approached, he noticed their arrival. With the ornate staff he held in his right hand, he gave two sharp raps.

The debate halted immediately.

"Our guests." The man who Sami assumed to be king lowered the tip of the staff toward Rook. "Nephew, please announce your human acquaintances."

"Sire," Rook responded. "Honored council." With a flourish, he waved his hand. "Allow me to introduce Tate, Sami, and

Fiona Whiteburn, known to many by their prophetic name. The daughters of Nadia."

A few grumbles and sounds of wonder met the announcement, but Rook continued, gesturing to each of the men. "Jack Helmsford, Ronan Gates, a soldier in service to the Dea Matrona, and Grayson LeRoux." Here Rook paused. "Also a soldier, in the human war against the bloodletting descendants of Malrik's breed."

Sami tensed her shoulders, unsure how the assembly would respond to a man whose sole purpose was the annihilation of their species' offspring.

Yet several of the council members nodded their approval, some even bestowing smiles on Grayson.

Sami's jaw went slack. But she recovered quickly and snapped her mouth shut.

*Didn't expect that.* Tate's voice flowed into Sami's head. She and her sisters rarely required their telepathic abilities, but it came in handy once in a while. Like now, when they might want to communicate without offending a king in his own castle.

*I don't know what to expect*, Sami sent back. Not all of the Iele of the council reacted kindly, and the glowers of a few told her they might resent the human visitors.

"So you bring more outsiders to our city," a man with icy-blue hair said. Though the Fae were immortal, his demeanor implied an Iele of some age, and entitlement. "You welcome more enemies of Malrik. You risk further inciting his wrath."

Jabbing a finger to the side of the room, the man ranted, "You go so far as to bring his daughter here with her oracle, drawing Malrik's eyes to our peaceful lands!"

His mention of Malrik's daughter had Sami looking to find Hellana. She stood just inside another doorway, her manner serene and patient.

Sami returned her attention to the king and council, where the fuming Iele still scorched Rook with his stare. "You are aware

Malrik pursues the seer with no concern for treaties or peaceful accords."

"We must hear what Rook has to say, Balwen." A female on the far left end spoke softly, though the gentle timbre held an undercurrent of steel. "We are here today to decide on a course of action. Let us not be premature."

Balwen showed his displeasure with a noisy harrumph but sat back in his chair.

"Well said, Arelia." The king addressed the female council member before holding out an open palm to Hellana. "Please forgive our rudeness, Queen Hellana." He didn't look at Balwen, but the reprimand was clear. "Won't you join the others and enlighten us with your knowledge of these matters?"

Slowly, regally, Hellana moved to the center of the room. She took up a position next to Rook. A soft, affectionate look passed between the two.

*Well, well.* Sami shared her thoughts with her sisters. *Not sure whether to congratulate Rook or warn him off.*

*I think we should hear what she has to say, too*, Fiona relayed.

*Always rooting for the underdog.* Sami almost grinned at the thought of her sister's romantic heart but managed to keep an appropriate expression in place.

"Honorable members of the council," Hellena began, "I want to first thank you for your hospitality. The generosity of the Vei Lanian people is truly boundless."

Stepping forward, she spread her hands. "Yet I also understand your concerns over my presence here, and the presence of Ayleen, the blind seer. What Your Honor said is true." She gestured to the annoyed Balwen. "Malrik does seek Ayleen. He wants to obtain her for her gift of sight, so much that he was willing to attack my kingdom."

Hellana sighed, hands clenched in the folds of a long, royal-blue skirt. "He attacked *me*, his own daughter." Her shoulders rolled back, a gesture of boldness. "I assure you there is no love lost between myself and the man who sired me, so you need not fear any allegiance on my part. He is a monster, and his rule is a blemish on the long and respectable history of the Ielonaar Realm."

Sami had no idea Hellana could be so eloquent. The woman was an onion, with many, many layers.

"Malrik is a fearsome warrior king, but lacks magick of his own," Hellana said. "This is why he makes captives of our realm's magick workers."

The cool and composed Arelia asked, "What do you mean?" just as a male on the council gasped and said, "He takes only those with power as his captives?" Clearly disturbed, he scooted forward on his chair ard tugged on the bottom of the silver doublet he wore.

At this, Hellana glanced at Rook.

In response, he spoke. "We all know Malrik has been waging war on other kingdoms of the realm, but because of our treaty with him, because we wanted continued safety," Rook nodded to Balwen when he said the last, "we ignored the destruction he wreaked on other lands. I fear that choice may now come back to destroy us."

When the council erupted with questions, the king only raised a hand. Quiet resumed, and Rook explained. "I believe Malrik has been raiding these kingdoms for a single purpose."

"To drink the blood of our brothers and sisters," a second female on the panel shouted, banging her fist on the arm of her chair.

"Yes," Rook agreed. "His warriors drink of their downed enemies." His features and his voice hardened. "And their vipera are allowed to feast."

Clasping his hands behind his back, Rook advanced to stand with Hellana. "But even if we ignore these atrocities, we can no longer deny that Malrik's main goal is to capture our realm's wizards, witches, and soothsayers. Any endowed with the gift of magick. He uses them to enhance his mighty army."

"But why?" the king asked, his brow furrowed. "He already controls so much. Why would he need magick?"

"Because you have it," Hellana stated plainly, to more muttering from Balwen and the male in the silver vest. "Malrik signed the treaty with your kingdom when he took my mother as his wife. But now he dishonors all agreements made in the past. He wants nothing more than to control the realm, to make Ielonaar one kingdom under his reign."

Her eyes beseeched the council to hear her. "Vei Lani is the last bastion of Iele decency, and the only thing standing in Malrik's way. Vei Lani is not a warring society, but it is a magickal culture."

"He needs power of his own to take us down." Rook laid it out in clear terms, his declaration stunning the council members to silence.

"He killed Emuirdane, my late husband, to consume the power in his blood." Hellana picked up where Rook left off and continued to persuade. "His lust for magick is also why he desired the Jeweled Ceffyl." She indicated Sami and her sisters. "But the daughters of Nadia freed the Ceffyl. Then they came here, to our world, to save my child. I trust them," she added. "As does Rook."

"I do," Rook agreed. "Which is why I believed they had a right to be here today. Though human, they battled Emuirdane in defense of their lives and their world. Now they must defend against Malrik as well. He is power-hungry, and his greed knows no bounds."

Rook drew himself up. "Which is why we must stop him."

"Absurd speculation!" Balwen cried. "How can you possibly know Malrik's intentions?"

"I know," Rook said, allowing a long, heavy pause to create tension. "I know, because I have a spy in his castle."

His declaration landed like rocks, and every face on the panel showed shock. All except the king's.

Hurrying on, Rook spoke in earnest. "The spy has sent a report confirming that a large contingent of Malrik's fighters left the barracks, only to return with new prisoners. All of these prisoners were magick workers, accompanied by select members of their families."

"How dare you!" Balwen stood, shaking his hands as he spoke. "You've placed a spy without our vote of consent." His furious tone turned imploring when he addressed the king. "Your Majesty, please. He endangers us all. Malrik will see this as an act of war!"

"Nonsense," the man in the silver vest said. "All of it is nonsense. Forgive me, Rook, but even with your foolhardy act, I do not believe Malrik would break the treaty." The councilman sniffed. "He would not dare attack us."

"He *would* care." A silky voice carried across the chamber, and all heads turned.

Fiona released a sharp breath. Tate narrowed her eyes fiercely. And Sami said, "Oh . . . *hell* no."

Grayson came to her side as if to protect her.

A Fae woman walked slowly into the great hall, her dove-gray dress sliding across the floor. Hair black as a raven and straight as rain fell to her waist, and crimson lips stood out in stark comparison to pale, pale skin.

Though her stride was elegant, her violet eyes flashed with indignation. "Malrik dares more than you know in his quest for power." She tossed a sneer to the council. "And you'd be wise to believe that he would attack you. Because, in his hubris, he *dared* attack me."

"Sami," Grayson said, leaning closer, "who is that?"

Disgust, rage, and fear churned in Sami's gut, but she forced a reply through clenched teeth. "Her name is Faidhia," she said in a brittle voice. "But most people call her the Winter Queen."

# 19

Sami planted her legs wide, braced for whatever the evil bitch might throw her way.

"You've allowed that lowborn knave to rise too high." The Winter Queen curled her upper lip as she reprimanded the council. "Malrik has gone unchecked for too long, and now he has gathered magickal power to add to his monstrous army of blood-drinkers."

"Faidhia," the king's gaze slid to Rook, "this is a surprise."

"Your nephew had the sense to welcome me, because I—unlike Malrik—still adhere to the Fae dictates of old. I only came here with Rook's invitation. But Malrik," here her rage broke free as she shook a fist, "he used a Dryys and sneaked into Faerie. With warriors!" she added in a shriek, now smashing both fists together.

"A dryys?" Grayson whispered.

"A portal," Sami answered, glad for his nearness. She did not fear Faidhia, but some serious Fae drama was currently unfolding. *Royal* Fae drama.

Faidhia's report of an assault on Faerie shone a new light on Malrik's arrogance. On exactly how far he was willing to go in his quest for dominance. And for the first time, even the king broke his facade of indifference, revealing emotion and expression that chilled Sami to the bone.

Because he looked afraid.

"That's where Malrik's troops went," Faidhia said, lowering

her voice. "To Faerie. They attacked my castle. They defeated my militia, as well as my spellcasters, because Malrik possesses his own."

Faidhia whirled suddenly, shooting daggers from her purple eyes at Sami and her sisters. "And you three caused it all."

The allegation plowed into Sami, so that she actually flinched. She shook her head, started to argue.

But the Winter Queen snarled at her, issuing a barrage in a language Sami didn't understand. Though she was pretty sure she was being insulted.

"You took the ring from Malrik, infuriating him and forcing him to find alternatives. Malrik's chasing bigger prizes now, making greater conquests." The queen thrust her hand toward Rook. "Ask him. It was only after you stole the ring from under Malrik's nose that he began to kidnap the magick makers."

"Malrik has been defeating other kingdoms for years, slowly gaining more strength." Rook rebutted Faidhia's claims. "Sami," he said, shaking his head. "Don't listen to her."

"No," was all Sami could muster, waiting for the guilt she'd defeated to rise, to rally inside of her.

"Oh, yes." Faidhia sent her a vicious smile. "You played where you did not belong. You and your sisters. *You* are the ones who woke the beast in Malrik. And now," her laugh rattled like stones over ice, "now he will consume us all."

*Don't let her get to you, Sami.* Tate's voice again. *Nothing she says matters.*

*No, it doesn't,* Sami replied mentally, realizing she felt no shame. No remorse. Not like she might have just days before. Before Grayson had pushed in his irritating way. Before he'd interrogated her about the ring.

Before he'd helped her to see reason.

So it was Grayson to whom she sent a smug grin, as she stepped up to face her accuser. "You're wrong, Faidhia."

The queen shoved out her chest. "I've not given you leave to address me with such familiarity."

"Actually, you told us *all* to call you by your first name." Fiona's tone was sugary, and all the more sarcastic for its sweet delivery. "Remember? When we were your guests in Faerie?"

Tossing a nod of thanks to Fiona, Sami jumped back in. "We shouldn't argue over formalities, Faidhia, because we are all facing the same problem, the same threat."

"Malrik," Rook supplied, crossing his arms and standing aside with Hellana, allowing Sami to take center stage.

"What Hellana said is true," Sami told the council and the king. "Malrik craves magick. He made a pact with Emuirdane, marrying off his daughter in return for the Jeweled Ceffyl. The artifact would have granted him one wish, and I have to believe he would have used that wish to gain magick. The one thing he does not have."

Sami shifted, focusing on the Winter Queen. "So you see, this is not our fault. Malrik began his pursuit of magick and power before my sisters and I were even born."

"But Malrik only started kidnapping Fae with mystical abilities *after* you took the ring from him."

"And what if I hadn't? What if he now controlled the ring?" Sami pressed on, echoing the very questions Grayson had thrown at her. "He would have more power than he does now, even with all of his captives."

Sami drew a deep, bolstering breath. "I admit, my actions changed the course of things. Malrik started gathering those who could do magick for him, because he didn't possess the combined strength of the ring and brooch. But with Emuirdane's gemstones, he would have been—"

"Unstoppable." The king spoke abruptly, bringing a pensive stillness to the vast hall. He rubbed a hand over his chin and stared into space. Finally, he met Sami's gaze. "Continue."

"Your Majesty." Sami bowed her head and swallowed, suddenly

appreciating the weight of the moment, and the boldness of her behavior.

But now was the time to be bold.

"Malrik will thirst for power no matter what we do. He will continue his attacks." Sami spoke directly to Balwen. "And none of us can turn a blind eye to his rampage. Not anymore."

Balwen repositioned in his chair but did not oppose her.

"Malrik is coming," Sami said. "We just have to decide how much power we allow him to gather before we stop him."

"We?" Faidhia scoffed. "Since when do humans concern themselves with the fate of the Fae?"

"Since we jumped through a portal to go to your world," Tate said, heat flaring with every word. "Since we braved the trials of Mount Aeylwon and risked our lives to find the Jeweled Ceffyl."

"We do not question your integrity." The king's statement brooked no argument as he shot the Winter Queen a silent admonition. "Nor do we question your valor."

Faidhia turned her head away and sniffed.

"Forgive my interruption." Grayson kept his tone respectful, but his right eye ticked, giving away his tension. "How was Malrik able to travel to Faerie?"

Rook pointed, as if he understood why Grayson had introduced the question. "You're wondering if he can enter your world as easily. But no, travel between Fae realms is different. Malrik would need great power to transport an army to where humans live. I believe that is why he wants the ring."

"And an oracle," Hellana added.

"Which is exactly why we can't allow him to have either," Sami said.

"Malrik's soldiers searched for my oracle." If possible, Faidhia's skin had grown whiter. "Her lair is underground, beneath the castle. The entrance was obscured by a spell. It's the only reason they didn't find her."

"With or without the ring, Malrik is making a play for power."
Arelia sat straighter in her chair. She remained calm, but lines of
worry creased her face. "We are one of the largest populations in
the realm, and magick runs through our blood."

"He could be coming here soon," Balwen said, no longer
blustering or argumentative.

"He's already taken the Skaar from Faerie." Rook's announcement
elicited more gasps. "We all know the threat those three mages
represent. And I believe . . ." Rook faltered and glanced at Hellana.

At her nod, he continued. "*We* believe Malrik will come here
next."

"Then we can't waste any more time." Balancing deference to
the king with her own determination, Sami lifted her chin. "It if
pleases Your Majesty, I'd like to help."

Confidence in her decision zipped through her system like bolts
of electricity. Now was the time to be bold. Now was the time to
stop Malrik. Before he murdered any more innocents, human or
Fae.

So decided, she faced Rook and made her pledge. "I'm going
to stay and fight."

~ ~ ~

Hours later, Grayson knocked on Sami's door. They'd all been
afforded guest rooms within the palace, and after the council
meeting and a long, formal Fae dinner, she'd begged off and made
herself scarce.

He assumed she'd come back to her chamber, the only place
in the kingdom she could be assured of privacy. But she didn't
respond, so he knocked again, louder and with more insistence.

"Come in." Her voice barely penetrated the thick wooden door.

Grayson entered and saw why. She wasn't in the suite, not
exactly, but standing outside on the balcony, leaning against the

stone balustrade.

Her deep auburn hair stirred in the breeze, and she still wore the outfit she'd been given for a formal meal in the palace. The gauzy skirt and stomach-baring top were both the color of aquamarine, embroidered with copper thread.

When she spun around to face him, she looked like a wild and exotic princess.

"This place is amazing," she said, reaching down behind the handrail. "Come see these flowers."

Forcing himself to ignore the romance of the situation—and the glimpse of her bare belly— Grayson joined her, peering over to see what had her so enthralled.

White blooms trailed across the side of the building. "They're like giant honeysuckle." She leaned out and sniffed. "Smell like them, too."

"Uh-huh," Grayson murmured, taking a whiff. Sami still smelled better.

"That was some dinner," he said, "the epitome of elegance." His eyes tracked to hers. "And I should have told you before, but you look beautiful."

She didn't blush, but she did look away with a light laugh. "I feel like it's Halloween, and the only thing I'm missing is my magic carpet."

Gripping the banister—because what he really wanted to do was trail his fingers down her stomach—Grayson switched gears, steering the conversation away from light banter and to the more serious issues at hand. "I spoke with Rook after the meal, and he said the council hasn't made a decision yet."

Sami shrugged. "I think they probably have, at least, most of them." She propped her elbows behind her. "But you can't blame them for taking a night to sleep on the idea. They'll be choosing war, for a society that has seen only peace for centuries. Iele years, which are a lot longer than ours."

"I get it." Grayson leaned on the railing beside her. "Even though war has filled my days for as long as I can remember, I get it. And I can't blame them."

Just like he couldn't blame her. Today Sami proved just how strong and fearless she really was, but the impact of her decision tangled his gut into knots. "So, you're staying," he said.

"Yes. So are my sisters, Jack, and Ronan. We asked Rook to contact Kat so she can let the rest of the family know." Still leaning back casually, she slanted gypsy-brown eyes his way. "LeRoux, if you want to go, I'll understand."

"Actually," he tapped his fist once, "I've decided to stay." There was a bite to his tone, but he couldn't help it.

"Why?" She pushed up and angled toward him. "I mean, why would you? I know how you feel about Iele, and that you only came for information."

"That's partly true, and I still despise the kind we fight back home. But, this place, these people . . . . I'll just say that the short time I've been here has been educational." He pictured the formerly murderous Hellana and how she'd cooed over her baby at dinner, along with another female he'd learned was Rook's cousin.

"I never thought I'd meet any Iele I could carry on conversations with. That I actually . . . like." He almost cringed to say it out loud. "It all seems so strange, so unreal. I know faeries can be masters of illusion, but the kindness of the people here seems genuine."

He stared up at the star-filled sky and two glowing moons. "Their behavior is so normal, filled with fear, hate, love." At a loss for how to express himself, he stole a move from Sami and simply shrugged.

"I know what you mean," she said. "Emuirdane and Hellana, the old, wicked version of Hellana, were my first introductions to the Fae. But really, the Iele have good and bad, weak and strong, just like us."

She touched his arm. "That's why I'm staying. I want to fight for the good, theirs and ours."

When he didn't respond, she returned to her laid-back position against the balustrade. "I guess you think I'm crazy, making a decision this big and this important on the basis of emotion. But personally, I think love, friendship, family, and all that go with them, are the only things worth fighting for."

"No, Sami. I don't think you're crazy at all." After the way she'd faced an Iele king, his council, and an old nemesis in the Winter Queen? Then chosen to stand her ground in a foreign world?

No. Not crazy. Stubborn, as ever. Yet also brave, unwavering, and selfless. Grayson raked a hand through his hair. *Just when I thought I couldn't be any more attracted to her.*

"So what happened, LeRoux?"

Still caught up in his internal struggle, he jerked his gaze to hers. "When?"

"In my workshop, you said emotions can kill, and you knew because you had firsthand experience."

For a brief moment, Grayson's mind went blank. The power of denial and a self-enforced custom of blocking out memories. Things too painful to recall.

But he felt the story surfacing, as if it needed to be freed as much as he wanted to let it out. With Sami, he could. Somehow, he knew he could.

"I was raised to fight and taught to kill." Giving in, Grayson let the wind carry his words safely to the sea. "My earliest memories are of my mother's love and my father's lessons. Control your emotions. Don't get distracted. Focus over feelings." He released a caustic sound. "He had so many expressions, constantly hitting me over the head with them. I swear, I heard them in my sleep."

He rubbed his palms over the coarse, gritty stone. "By the time I turned eighteen, I was going out with a team, using my skills to track Iele." Now he kicked back his head and shook it slowly. "God, I was cocky. I thought I knew it all, and that I could handle anything."

When Sami's hand touched his, he turned his over to curl their fingers together. "I fell in love, or in lust. You know when they both collide at that age, and it's the greatest, most overpowering thing you ever knew?"

"I do," she whispered.

"She was on my team." He paused, and made himself go on. "One night, we tracked a vamp back to a nest. At least eight living together in this old Southern mansion out near the swamp." Grayson's chest clutched at the memory. He could still hear the frogs calling, still feel the heavy moisture of a summer night in Louisiana.

Then the heat turned cold as he remembered the mistake. The one that had cost lives.

"Her name was Laura. She'd scaled up to the second story and onto a terrace." He rubbed his face, as if he could force the regret from his mind. "We should have called it in, but we thought we could handle it ourselves."

"Tell me," Sami urged. "All of it."

"Laura stepped on a loose board, a loud creaky board. Three were in an upstairs room. They heard her. They were on her so fast—"

"God, Grayson. I'm sorry. You lost your first love."

"No." He jolted. "I mean, yes, I guess. But as heartless as it sounds, her death was a result of the choice we all made. The *mistake* we all made together. What happened next was because of me."

Disgust churned in his stomach like a ball of vipers. Disgust for himself. "I knew she was gone. I saw how many had her, and I saw when she stopped moving. She was dead. But I broke protocol and went up to her, even though other vamps were spilling from the house."

He faced Sami. "Three more of my team died that night, because

I let my feelings for someone override a lifetime of preparation—exercise, training, drills. My father's mantras. All of them flew out of my head, because I let emotions distract me."

"You can't be sure—"

"Yes, I can. That's the point of running through every possible scenario. If I'd done what I'd been taught to do and left the dead to help the living, I know we would have had fewer casualties."

For a moment, silence was heavy between them. Then Sami tilted her head. "That's why you lean on logic and rational decisions." She took his hand again, and held tight.

"I have responsibilities, and I have to make sound decisions. Since that night, I have. I've been able to trust my own judgment." He lifted one hand to cup Sami's cheek. "Until you."

She leaned into his palm, and he couldn't help smoothing it down her neck to the valley of her shoulder. "You unbalance me, Sami. You confuse me. I have to stop and question my every choice."

"I don't understand." She seemed suddenly subdued, her tone soft and unsure.

"I came here to represent my organization and gain intel, for the sake of the human race. And I'm staying, because you're right. To protect our people, we have to stop Malrik here, in this realm."

His fingers curled into the soft fabric of her top. "I know that's what I should do. What I must do."

"But?" A small wrinkle formed between her eyebrows.

"But every fiber of my being wants to leave, only so I can drag you out of here and away from what we both know is coming." He eased closer, dropping his forehead to hers. "I've learned to suppress my feelings and my own needs, but now, when I want to give in the most, I just can't. I can't steal you away and take you somewhere you'll be protected from all of this."

A palpable force seemed to pull him to her. "As much as it kills me, I have to accept that you'll be fighting an army of soulless beasts right by my side. Because you're a powerful witch, an amazing warrior, and we all need you here."

He slid his hand into her riotous curls. "But I still want you gone. I want you *safe*."

"We both know that's not going to happen." Her arms encircled his waist. "So what else do you want?"

"Sami," he shook his head.

"Don't." She kissed him lightly. "Don't deny. Don't overanalyze. Just let this be what it's going to be. We've both decided to stay, and neither of us knows just how bad this war is going to get. So we should live now. We should take what we can. What we want."

She hiked one long leg up, bare and golden, and stroked it slowly back down his. "I certainly can't deny you." Her breath hitched as she spoke. "Not after you called me an amazing warrior."

She closed in to skim her lips along his jaw. "I think that's the sexiest thing a man has ever said to me."

The purr of her voice shot straight to his loins, so he shushed her with two fingers over her lips. Gently. Seductively.

Easing back, he studied her flushed cheeks and gorgeous eyes, the brown gone even darker with desire. The pulse in her neck fluttered so prettily he longed to cover it with his mouth. To feel her throb against his tongue.

"You want to kiss me again," she challenged.

"More than I want to breathe." His voice had grown husky.

"Then for once, don't think." Putting her hands on his hips, she gave one quick tug and brought his lower body against hers. "Just act."

His erection pressed to her heat, and all logic disappeared. All inhibitions fled. And doubt no longer had a place between them.

He held her trapped against the balustrade as he moved in—with his hips, with his mouth—and she went pliant in his arms. He lowered his lips to her neck, felt her throb, then bared her shoulder to taste her there.

She sighed his name when his hands slid down her body. Quivered when he lifted her skirt. And moaned when his fingers skimmed up her thigh, moving to the juncture of her legs to tease.

"I wouldn't have expected panties," he said, "not with this outfit."

"They're sheer. Practically see-through."

"Then I'm taking you inside and into the light, where I can see every inch as I—"

Screams cut through the night.

He and Sami both tensed, looked at each other, and started to run.

"The courtyard," he said as they moved. "They're coming from the courtyard."

# 20

Sami raced after Grayson through the corridors of the palace. With his speed, she couldn't keep pace, but she'd already yelled for him to go.

To just *go*.

Swinging through an arched doorway, they took one of the central staircases they'd seen on their tour of the opulent building. While Grayson all but flew down the winding steps, Sami jumped the rail and used her telekinesis to float quickly to the bottom.

In a heartbeat, they were out the doorway and running down the main corridor that led to the rear of the palace and the courtyard outside. As one, they burst through the doors.

And entered pure bedlam.

Through the open gates of the courtyard walls, Sami could see the people of Vei Lani scattering, yelling and shouting as they ran.

One woman stood rooted in her spot under a towering palm tree inside the walls. Screaming, her terrified gaze remained locked on two doormen struggling to beat back a hulking Iele with blood dripping down his chin.

A vampire. Not just any vampire, but an original. With all the strength and speed afforded to the Fae.

The bloody monster hissed and punched at the doormen, standing over a form crumpled between his spread legs. From the white and blue dress, Sami recognized one of the young women who worked in the palace.

*Too late.* Sami's stomach dropped out. The girl on the ground was already dead.

More calls and shouts rose from beyond the courtyard, coming from the streets. Just then, the woman beneath the palm pointed up and screamed, "Vipera! Vipera are coming!"

Sami and Grayson searched the sky, and she thought she caught a glimpse of a dark shape blotting out the stars. Even as she stared, a figure fell from the flying serpent.

Another huge Iele, dressed in battle gear, landed in a crouch. And roared.

"By the gods!" Hellana rushed up beside Sami with Rook close behind. "The flying beasts are dropping Malrik's men."

Like weapons, Sami thought. Living bombs, landing with an explosion of fangs, claws, and swords.

Grayson launched himself at the vampire who'd killed the girl, and Rook dashed toward the one who'd just hit the ground. So Sami bolted out the side gate to help whoever was being attacked in the street.

She spotted another of Malrik's brutes, but he was down on one knee, one arm raised in an attempt to fend off the three Vei Lanian men surrounding him. Each took a turn stabbing at him with curved blades, scimitar-style weapons glinting with gold and jewels.

"They're using gold," Sami said in astonishment.

"Of course." Hellana had joined her again. "What else?"

"But it's poison to Iele, including the people here."

"Yes. But can't humans be killed by the guns and knives they wield?"

"Yeah. Sure." Sami nodded. "I guess I see what you mean."

"We cover the handles with illuseian, a protective substance." While she spoke, Hellana scanned the city, as did Sami.

Citizens were returning from shelter and pouring back into the streets, weapons in hand. Even with the crowds growing again, the commotion seemed to subside. The cries of alarm lessened, and so did the roars of violence and shrieks of pain.

Occupants of the city milled outside, now prepared for an enemy who was no longer breaching the safety of their lands.

"It was over so quickly," Hellana said.

"Yeah," Sami murmured. But something didn't feel right. "Let's go back."

Rook waited in the gateway, an odd expression marring his brow. Confusion or upset, Sami couldn't tell.

"Grayson?" she asked, lurching ahead of Hellana.

"He's fine," Rook said. "He's not hurt."

Still, she hurried inside the courtyard. Staring down at a dead vampire, Grayson wiped his dagger on his pant leg and turned.

A strange sensation spread inside Sami's chest. She ran to him and threw her arms around his neck.

His hand rose to cradle the base of her head and pressed her cheek to his. "I hate this," he said, running his palm up and down her back.

She pulled away, searching the depths of his dark eyes. "I know. I was worried about you, too. I never expected . . ."

In lieu of the words she couldn't find, she put her lips to his.

"I didn't expect this either," he said, his breath shuddering from his body. He gently lowered his forehead to hers, as he had on the balcony. The tender gesture made her heart trip over itself.

One hand still on her waist, he pulled away and glanced around. "This feels wrong." He looked past her to Rook as he reentered the courtyard. "No more on the streets?"

"No. And my men just reported that the gardens and beach are clear." He shook his head.

"Has anyone seen my sisters?" Sami said, a new fear squeezing her throat.

"Hellana and I spoke to them," Rook said, "only moments before we heard the clamor and came out here. Fiona wanted to see the kitchens again, so she and Tate went down with one of the cooks."

He continued in a tone meant to placate. "I'm sure they're safe. The kitchens are always loud, at any hour day or night. You can't hear things easily from there."

Sami accepted his reassurance.

"Why a sneak attack if they were only going to drop a few fighters?" Grayson asked to no one in particular.

"Yes. And they were overrun in minutes." Rook put his hands on his hips and studied one of the dead creatures sprawled in a twisted form across a flower bed. "They basically sacrificed themselves. But why?"

Grayson's jaw ground hard enough to bulge at the sides. "To create a distraction."

"Their dropping from the sky like that was terrifying." Sami stood apart from Grayson as her mind whirred. "So people panicked and screamed."

"And everyone else came running, including us." Grayson looked up at the palace's glowing windows. "It's quiet in there. Maybe too quiet."

Sami curled her fingers into her palms. It occurred to her at the same moment as Grayson. "The oracle," they said in unison.

Hellana made a sound of pain. "She and Velloria are in their chamber." Staring at the palace, she cried, "I left Keaghan with them!"

At once, they all fled back inside, Hellana leading the way with a burst of maternal strength as they sprinted past curious onlookers peeking out of doors. Together, the four of them thundered up the stairs.

"Which way?" Grayson slowed on the upper level, only to have Rook and Hellana blast ahead of him and down the passage to the right.

A loud crash followed by the sound of splintering wood ricocheted in the halls, and they rounded the corner in time to see three of Malrik's men disappear into a room.

"No!" Hellana increased her speed, but Rook and Grayson both beat her to the broken door.

Sami readied her fire, internally ramping up her power. She could hear grunts and snarls coming from inside as she skidded to a halt and scanned the chamber.

Grayson and a vampire circled each other while Rook stabbed and sliced at a second fiend.

Hellana pushed through the door. "Get away, you beast!" She rushed toward the third soldier, who was advancing on two older women in a corner of the room.

One of the women had empty sockets where her eyes should have been. The oracle. She let her arms hang limply at her sides, seemingly unaffected by the chaos in her living quarters.

The other woman, Velloria, held a vase in her raised hands, likely the first object she'd been able to grab. Legs spread, she squared off with the brute, protecting the bassinet behind her.

Tiny cries and whimpers rose up to mingle with the noise of ongoing brawls.

"Hellana," Sami called, fearing the woman would rush headlong into danger, "you need a blade."

Focused only on her child, Hellana ignored her and lunged toward the vampire's back.

Sensing her attack, he whirled and lifted his hand, covered in a metal gauntlet with razor-sharp points.

Sami thrust out her hand, and with it, her magick. The heat of power rolled up from her gut, boosted by fear, terror over what those vicious knives could do to the three women.

Or to a helpless baby.

The soldier froze in place, paralyzed mid-swing, unable to break from Sami's hold.

Grayson finished off the fiend he'd been sparring with, jabbing his dagger—Sami's gift—into the creature's chest. Then he shouted

Hellana's name.

Hellana whipped in Grayson's direction, lifted her hand, and caught the weapon he threw to her. Pivoting back, she plunged the gold-marbled blade into the heart of the foolish monster who'd threatened her child.

As soon as the vampire collapsed, she dropped the dagger and stared at her palm.

"Are you poisoned?" Velloria asked, setting aside the vase to inspect Hellana's hand.

"No." Hellana leaned between the two women to check on Keaghan. "I only held it for an instant."

Sami blew out through pursed lips. The baby was safe.

Relief was sweet but brief as Rook's cry of pain jerked their attention to him. The soldier he'd fought had fallen and appeared to be dying.

But he'd landed a blow, the sharp blades of his metal glove carving through Rook's shoulder.

"Rook." Hellana gasped his name and took a step. She paused to look back at her baby.

"I've got him," Velloria said.

Assured of her son's safety, Hellana was at Rook's side in an instant.

~~~

Pain ripped into Rook's arm and chest as he let himself settle to the carpet in a heap. He pressed his hand to the wound and came away with blood.

Shocked by the red liquid coating his palm, he could only stare.

Hellana dropped down next to him and cupped his face between her hands. "Rook, look at me." She turned his head. "Let me see your eyes."

Blinking, he cleared his vision and focused on her face. Her glorious face. "Hellana." His breath left him in a rush.

When her mouth rounded with concern, he said, "I'm all right. I think I'll be all right." Yet he winced when he tried to move his arm. "Keaghan?" he asked, trying to sit up.

"He's safe." Hellana held him down. "But you need a healer."

"Better send for one."

"No. Velloria's here. She's the best." Her soft hands touched his face again. Her soft lips brushed with his. And when she leaned back, her blue eyes were suspiciously moist. "You will only have the best."

Velloria came to stand behind Hellana. "Let me see to him, my dove." Beyond the nurse, Rook saw Sami holding the baby, Grayson's hand resting on her shoulder.

Rook relaxed, certain the child would be well guarded. The child he was growing to love. And as for his mother . . .

"Hellana," Rook grimaced, "my shoulder pains me." When her features fell into lines of worry, he said, "I think you need to kiss me again."

Sitting back on her knees, Hellana sent him a scolding yet playful look. "No. No need for that," she teased as she stood to let the nurse take her place. "I can see you're already feeling better."

# 21

Sami toweled off her shower-damp hair, delighting in the light, fruity scent of Iele shampoo. She'd never considered herself a "girly" girl but was maybe beginning to see the merits. She might even get used to luxury, to the finer things she'd never paid much heed.

But only—she told herself, caressing the silky peach-colored robe she wore—only after *all* worlds were free from the threat of Malrik.

And that would take hard work, rigorous training, and painful sacrifice. Thinking of pain, she skimmed her fingertips over the blisters forming on her right hand, her dominant fighting hand.

Days had passed since Malrik's devious air raid and attempt to kidnap the oracle. After the unexpected assault, Vei Lani's king and council had unanimously come to a decision. A difficult decision they'd then announced to their once-peaceful citizenry.

Negotiations were no longer an option, compromise no longer a valid choice. The people of Vei Lani would return to ancient ways, to practices laid to rest centuries before. They would pick up spear and shield. They would re-fire the forge. They would rebuild the watchtowers.

And they would go to war.

The Vei Lanians weren't the only ones learning new tricks and building new muscles. Sami and her sisters trained as well, working like demons alongside Jack, Ronan, and Grayson, each man with his own unique skills to offer.

As it turned out, there were many who wanted to benefit from Jack's art of blade-throwing, Ronan's experience commanding troops, and—Sami pictured with a grin—Grayson's deadly hand-to-hand combat moves.

All of them, human and Iele, had been pressing hard day and night. Hence the new blisters on her sore, aching body.

She studied the painful bubble on her left hand as well, from her mediocre attempts to become ambidextrous. Grimly, she reflected on the rules she and her sisters followed.

The first and most sacred—Harm none. Well that one was out, but for good reason.

Next—The rule of three. Borrowed from the Wiccan rede, meaning whatever you send out in energy, you may get back threefold. One reason Sami never messed around with love spells. Why invite a stalker?

And last—Never use magick for self-advancement.

Sami mulled this one over and considered the high stakes of the current situation. She curled her fingers, felt the sting of blisters and . . . *Screw it.* Closing her eyes, she channeled healing energies throughout her body.

Sensing the ache of her muscles beginning to dissipate, she opened her eyes to watch the blisters fade. She shrugged. With the fate of multiple worlds at stake, she figured the energies of the universe would give her a pass.

Wiggling her much happier fingers, she stepped out onto the balcony to enjoy the view. Sure, the sunset over the sea was amazing, but that wasn't the view she'd been imagining.

Below on the white sands, Grayson led a sparring class. Having worked up a sweat in the mild humidity, as he did most days, he'd stuck with habit and taken off his shirt.

Leaning forward on her elbows, Sami interlaced her hands. And simply watched.

She'd known he was in prime physical condition, and she'd felt his steely strength for herself. But seeing him in action—muscles rippling and dark eyes fierce—sent another kind of energy sizzling through her system.

Not only had it been days since the attack, but also days since she and Grayson had enjoyed any intimate time together. There was just so much to do, so much to learn, if they intended to be ready for Malrik's next attack.

Acts of preparation filled every long, grueling hour of the days and nights. So the few times she and Grayson met in the evenings, it was often for a brief kiss or a shared meal.

Before they both collapsed into their respective beds.

Eyeing his sleek power and fluid grace, Sami contemplated casting a spell for extra energy. *Nah. That might be pushing it.*

She doubted the universe would give her a pass for curing sexual frustration.

A quick *tock-tock-tock* sounded from her chamber door before Fiona and Tate barged in. "Hey, have you eaten?" Tate asked, an efficiency in her tone and manner telling Sami she was plotting something.

"I grabbed a plate from the kitchens." Sami notched her chin to the silver disc, now covered only in crumbs. "Why? What's up?"

"We just had a chat with Rook," Fiona said, green eyes sparkling with mischief as she plopped down in a poppy-red chair. "Remember when he and Kat linked hands over that bowl of water?"

Sami angled her head. "Yeah. You mean when they did some psychic spying on Malrik?" She had an idea what they were thinking, and she was totally on board. Grayson would be training his Vei Lanian students for a while anyway. "So what's the plan?"

"Rook thinks we should go bigger," Tate said. "Now that we're here in Vei Lani, Rook has access to others who also have his gift of perception. He went to speak with the two he has in mind."

"And he wants us to be the other three." Fiona crossed her legs and wiggled her toes.

"Us?" Sami lifted her shoulder. "We aren't water witches."

"No, but we do have power," Tate said, "and a degree of psychic ability." She cocked a hip and waved her hand as she postulated. "Plus, we'd be a different type of mystical . . . *source*, for lack of a better word. The combined magick of human and Iele could boost the, um . . ."

"Signal," Fiona finished for her. "And it might also help cover our tracks. Malrik might be expecting Rook's people to go poking around."

"But not us. Not from here." Sami nodded, thinking back to the night vampires literally fell from the sky. "None of the soldiers he sent survived, so there was no one to tell Malrik we're here in the Ielonaar Realm."

"Dead vamps tell no tales." Tate's face was sober and serious.

Until all three of them burst into giggles.

"There's always the chance one of Malrik's magick slaves could sense our presence, but odds are good he doesn't have anyone with the gift of sight. Or else, he wouldn't still be searching for an oracle."

"Then we're in?" Fiona asked, knees bouncing.

"We're in." Sami tugged at the belt of her robe. "Just let me get dressed."

Minutes later, she and her sisters strolled through the sumptuous corridors of the palace. Following the route Rook had suggested, they exited through a curtained doorway to an outside terrace. Pillowed seats scattered here and there, for lounging amongst thick pillars covered with curling green vines.

Traipsing down sandstone steps, the three of them entered what Rook had called the hanging gardens. Here, more of the verdant lianas spread over palace walls, as well as the top of long arbors used to shade pebbled paths.

An open gate led them toward the beach, where Rook waited with two other Vei Lanians, a man and a girl who looked like a teenager.

"We have a kettle of ebonite," Rook said, indicating a large black basin filled with water. The cauldron stood out against the ivory sand, while its water reflected a twilight sky.

"Ebonite?" Tate asked, ever inquisitive.

"A mineral to enhance psychic travel and perception." He looked out over the ocean where white caps rode a darkening sea. "The ocean will help as well. Our magick comes from the water, and her great soul is mighty and deep."

His reverence for the sea sent chills over Sami's arms. Not out of fear, but of the sense they were about to call upon a divine entity.

"This is Makel." Rook introduced the man who inclined his head in greeting. "And our young mystical prodigy, Della." He sent a proud smile to the younger female. "She has quite the talent for flying. Spiritually, that is."

"Tisu," Della said. "I am honored to do magick with the daughters of Nadia."

"We are honored as well," Fiona said softly.

When Della grinned, Fiona moved to stand with the girl. "So, should we have humans on one side and Iele on the other or," she offered her hand, "should we mix it up?"

"Mixing is good." Della stood taller and brushed the long strands of her turquoise hair over her shoulders. Then she clasped hands with Fiona.

Following suit, Sami intertwined fingers with Rook on her right and Della on her left as Tate positioned herself between the two men. Lastly, Makel and Fiona completed the circle.

Assuming Rook would speak—as he had the last time in the kitchen of her family home—Sami drew a long cleansing, calming breath, and opened herself to the wonder of sight.

She could actually feel the rest of her circle doing the same and knew the instant they had all connected. A stream of tingling warmth ran through her, and as she closed her eyes, she could envision them surrounded by a sparkling blue ring of light.

"May our minds travel and our secret eyes seek." The heavy timbre of Rook's voice raised to meet the wind. "With our bodies bound, our consciousness free, take us through tortured lands and over mountain peak. Guide our vision to Castle Sangridor, and keep us from their sight, to the darkness surrounding King Malrik, let us travel through the night."

Sami sensed herself lifting, weightless and buoyant, though her feet still sank into the sand. She still saw the circle of blue light in her mind, but it began to flicker, like a fluorescent bulb about to die.

"May our minds travel and our secret eyes seek." Rook spoke the words again, but this time he sounded strained, as if having to force each syllable.

*This isn't how Kat described it.* Keeping her eyes closed, Sami struggled to remain calm, to stay open.

"Pull back, Rook," Della urged, the young girl emanating a sense of panic and fear. "Pull back!"

Suddenly, a powerful surge swept Sami up, as if the sky above had jerked her on a chain. And just as quickly, she hit a barrier, slamming into an obstacle she couldn't see.

Pain shattered inside her head, and starbursts exploded behind her closed lids.

"Break! Break!" Della's high-pitched cries registered to Sami, but she couldn't see anything. She couldn't feel her body. Desperately, she wanted to grab at her head, to pull out the spikes jamming into her brain.

"Just sit, Fiona. Just sit down." Della spoke again, her voice the only thing Sami could hear. "Makel, break free." The girl issued another command.

Static roared all around. Was it the wind? The ocean? Had they infuriated a god?

*Help me. Find me.* The plea issued from Sami's subconscious, though she no longer knew where she was or whom she begged. All she could see, hear, feel, taste was lightning-sharp agony behind her eyes.

"Sami." The gentle voice returned like a cooling balm. "Sami, let go of Rook's hand."

She felt an insistent tug on her fingers.

"Sami, let go!"

With an audible *crack!* the pain released, and Sami could see clearly again. She realized she lay partially in the sand, knees folded beneath her and one elbow propped up. Her mind depleted. Her body exhausted.

Massaging her temple, Sami looked up at Della. "What was that? What did we do?"

"Not us." Della bent to grip Sami's chin softly and stare into her eyes. "You got the worst of it. I'm sorry. You were the last to break. You and Rook." She glanced over and Sami tracked her line of sight.

Rook kneeled, his head cradled between his palms.

"Thank the gods for you, Della." Makel rubbed the center of his chest. "If you hadn't been here. If you hadn't pulled us out . . ."

"Yes." Rook gained his feet, but he wobbled. "You saved us. I should have known better, but . . ."

"You can't blame yourself." Della folded her arms primly. "We had to try." She released a sigh rife with annoyance. "But we mustn't try again. Malrik employs a mighty conjurer, an illusionist possibly, or a wizard." She scowled. "Whoever it is, his practice is of the dark arts."

"Is that what I hit?" Slowly, Sami rolled to her knees, paused for a few seconds, and stood.

Tate took Sami's elbow to help keep her steady. "You okay?"

Sami almost nodded, but then thought better of it. "I'll be fine.

I'm starting to clear up, but if this is a magickal hangover, I might have to go on the wagon."

"What wagon?" Makel asked.

Reluctant and low, Sami's laughter helped chase the last painful dregs from her skull. "I'll tell you all about it," she said, still holding on to Tate. "Just as soon as I can think straight again."

"We should all rest," Della said, her authoritative tone drawing smiles from Rook, Makel, and Fiona. "And eat."

"Agreed." Rook scanned the group. "Thank you all for trying. We didn't succeed, not as we'd hoped, but we did gain new information." He used both hands to dump the water from the cauldron. "At least we know more of our enemy's strength."

"And that's the last we'll learn, for now." This from Makel. "We won't dare spy on Malrik again, not with whatever magician he's got guarding his gates."

The circle of six accepted this in silent agreement.

"Let's get you to your room," Fiona said, taking Sami's opposite arm.

Sami didn't have the will to argue. "Sounds good." Saying their goodnights, the three of them made an unhurried trek across the sand.

Dancing flames caught her eye, and she stopped. Grayson continued to practice with others farther down the beach, their training now done by the light of hanging torches.

His body glistened under firelight as he demonstrated a kick.

With a sigh of regret, Sami accepted the loss of another night. And with her sisters helping her every step, she made her way up to her lonely bed.

# 22

Castle Sangridor
The Ielonaar Realm

"What does he want?" Malrik demanded of his emissary. Alongside Vale, he stalked through the lower level of the castle, an area caught somewhere between the security of the servants' quarters above and the misery of the dungeons below.

"He only said he has news to report and," Vale huffed as if mightily aggrieved, "that he will only report to you."

"Then he should hope his news is significant enough to pull me away from my meal." While in his study overlooking a proposed plan of action, Malrik had been slaking his bone-deep thirst with a chalice of fresh, warm blood.

Upon his approach, Malrik flicked a finger. The guard outside the door scrambled to make way.

Malrik marched into the room, and instantly became disoriented. "Ogin, by the gods!" He threw a hand up to shield his eyes from the tower of fire in the center of the chamber. And the hundreds of broken mirror shards reflecting the green flames.

"Forgive me, Your Majesty." With a snap of fingers, the wizard clouded each mirror with a dense pewter haze. But left the emerald flames dancing. "Had you been announced," he added with a sneer for the guard, "I would have been more considerate."

"You mean *respectful*," Malrik suggested, eyes narrowing. The wizard was ever pushing the boundaries, testing his position among Malrik's more valued minions.

Ogin's bizarre eyes—like fog with a whisper of green—curved upward at the corners in accompaniment of his smug, arrogant smile. As the only magick worker here by choice instead of coercion, the wizard continued to plead his case for advancement.

"If you've asked to see me for another request to move you upstairs . . ."

"No, Your Majesty." Ogin placed pointed fingertips to his chest and inclined his head. "Your time is far too valuable to waste."

Breathing through his nose, Malrik crossed his arms. "What have you?"

Long black cloak trailing on the dirty cobblestones, Ogin slithered to the leaping fire. "I have thwarted an attempt to infiltrate your kingdom, sire. It seems the Vei Lanians did not take kindly to your latest maneuver."

Reminded of the failure—of losing the oracle *yet again*—Malrik forced his hands behind his back so as not to throttle the presumptuous conjurer. "Watch your tone, Ogin. You may be here of your own free will, but you can still be replaced."

"Of course, sire. I only meant to say the Vei Lanians have responded. Using their powers of water, they tried to enter your lands, to violate the privacy of your castle."

"They would spy on me." Malrik glowered at the sharp points of Ogin's green pyramid of fire.

"And . . ." the wizard's voice held a teasing quality.

"Yes," Malrik snapped. "What else?"

"I sensed another presence, one not of Fae origin." Ogin curled the fingers of one hand as if catching a fly in the air. "Witches, sire. Human witches." He smiled broadly now. "You know the three of whom I speak."

Rage tightened in Malrik's chest until he felt his ribs would crack. The cursed, thieving sisters who'd freed the Jeweled Ceffyl, stolen his ring, and continued to defeat the men he sent to the human world. 'I will peel their pretty white flesh and—"

Mid-curse, Malrik halted. "The sisters joined with Vei Lanians." Ogin nodded.

"They were unsuccessful."

"I swore to guard all that is yours with my life's breath." Ogin spread his hands and simpered.

"But where were they? Where are they now?" Malrik stepped closer. "The witches?"

"Here in our realm. They are in Vei Lani."

"Hmm." Malrik prowled the dark chamber as he processed the import of this new development. "With their combined power, they could not get past. They could not see."

Putting a fist to his chin, Malrik stopped pacing and considered the smarmy wizard. He reassessed. "Well done, Ogin. It's possible I underestimated you." He pointed at him. "Keep this up, and you may soon find yourself housed in more comfortable surroundings."

"It is ever my pleasure to serve, sire." Now he bowed, his long, greasy black hair draping over one shoulder.

Malrik drew near the flames. The flickering fire was cold, cold and mesmerizing. "How certain are you they can't get through? That they can't guess our intentions?"

Ogin pulled up as if offended. "Positive, sire."

"Good." Malrik stepped away rubbing his palms together. "Very good." A cruel smile crawled over his face, and a dark thrill spurted in his veins. "They will never see us coming."

# 23

Sami followed the trail through the jungle, carrying a towel and change of clothes over her arm. She could tell she wasn't that far inland, as the sound of waves rushing up to the shore still drifted through the huge palm trees.

Casually, she wound her way along the path, taking time to investigate waxy leaves as large as eagle wings or to smell bold orange blossoms swaying in the breeze. She could do so without worry now, since Rook had assured her Vei Lanian plants posed no danger.

She passed the flag on a pole, as Rook had told her to expect. A bright green banner flapped gently, the color notifying others that the hot springs were already in use.

She paused and listened. Rook had said the springs were clear. That's why he'd sent her now.

"Hello?" She waited for an answer, then crept a few feet closer. She still heard nothing. "Anyone in there?" Only silence. Shrugging, she decided to take a chance, assuming the last person had just forgotten to change the flag.

Since she'd be using the springs now, she left the banner as it was.

Sore from head-to-toe, she was almost desperate for a hot, relaxing soak, so she eased her way around the bend. And almost cried with joy.

The three connected pools were of various sizes, round in shape, and filled with water in a pure perfect blue. Rook had promised the hot springs would do her good, both the heat and minerals serving to ease her aches.

But he'd failed to mention he'd directed her to paradise. Dropping her clean clothes and towel on a patch of grass, she began to undress.

Grateful for the system, since she planned to get naked, Sami quickly stripped, dumped the soiled clothing in a pile, and hurried to the edge of the nearest pool. Dipping her foot, she released an "Ahhh," then eased down to the edge and lowered herself in.

After dunking her hair and washing her face, she let her head fall back and enjoyed the bliss. Pure bliss—birds calling, water soothing, and tropical scents flowing in Vei Lani's version of Eden's garden.

She back-stroked from the first small pool into the larger one in the center, and on to the last where she flipped and dove to the bottom. She found a smooth, round rock the color of Turquoise, and shot back up.

She surfaced to soothing jungle sounds. And footsteps, a heavy tread coming down the path.

"The flag!" she called, for lack of anything more coherent.

In answer, the footsteps stopped, then resumed in a faster pace before a grinning Grayson strode into view. "I thought I recognized your voice." He quirked his mouth to one side. "Although, that may be the first time I've ever heard you so panicked."

Splashing water at him, though he was far away, Sami laughed despite herself. "I wasn't panicked. Not really." She briefly dropped her chin and lips into the blue liquid. "But the flag was out. Why didn't you stop? I could have been an eighty-year-old Vei Lanian woman."

"You put out the wrong flag. It was green, so I changed it to white."

"Rook told me green when he sent me."

"Well," Grayson pulled open the snap on his pants, "he told me white when he sent *me*. White means occupied. I only came because you'd left out the green."

"I wonder why Rook said—" Sami connected the dots, and she had to laugh. "I think Rook is playing matchmaker. That explains why he insisted I try the springs. Right *now*."

"And then came straight to me and told me to take a break." Grayson hiked a brow. "He was pretty demanding, said I'd be of no use in battle if I had a tired, sore body."

Pants undone to reveal a tempting trail of dark hair, Grayson pulled off his dark gray shirt. Then he looked down at her, and the grin he wore was pure wickedness. "Remind me to buy Rook a present sometime."

He untied his boots, jerked them off, and hooked his thumb under the waistband of his pants.

He held there. "You want to turn around?" he asked.

Sami shook her head. "Nope." She bit her bottom lip, dragging her gaze down his body in a lecherous way. "But I will do this." Giving him a short reprieve, she slipped beneath the water and stayed there. At least until she heard his splash into the center pool.

She popped back up again, searching for Grayson. Her breath lodged in her lungs when she found him. Midnight black, his hair shone with wet, his bronze skin all but glistening. And his eyes— the dark intensity, the scorching heat—caused a long, liquid pull in her belly.

His gaze dropped, and she would swear she felt his stare on her skin. She had to force words past the flutter in her chest. "Getting a good look, Grayson?"

He continued toward her, easing through the water. "I'm doing my best."

Teasing, taunting, she backed away. "Is looking all you want?"

He lunged fast, like a big cat landing on its prey. And before she could evade, he had her cornered against the natural wall of the spring.

Holding himself back, just a few inches away, he traced a fingertip over the tops of her breasts. "Have I mentioned what you do to my self-control?"

Shivering beneath the light touch, she met his gaze. "You seem like you're in control to me."

"That's what I want you to see." Under the water, he circled a fingertip around her belly button. "But if you knew what I was thinking," he skimmed up, glided that finger between her breasts, and to the small notch at the base of her throat.

"If you knew what I wanted to do to you." Moving up to cup her face, he held her steady and closed in. "You might realize exactly what I'm holding back."

With his lips brushing hers, she whispered, "Then don't." She nipped at his bottom lip. "Don't hold back."

With a fierce growl, he crushed his mouth to hers, and she all but exploded from the sweet, wet contact. Shattered by need, she lifted her hips, caught up in the rhythm of an ancient dance.

Impatient for him now, she ran her hands down his shoulders and his deliciously hard back.

He dropped his mouth to the side of her neck, paying special attention to the hollow beneath her jaw.

"Sami." He said her name in a hoarse voice before he pulled away.

"Don't stop." From beneath heavy lids, she sent him a warning look. "If you stop, I'll have to hurt you."

"Not stopping." His grin was sinful. "No chance in hell."

Locking his arms around her waist, Grayson lifted her so his naked chest was in full contact with hers. On a groan he plunged his tongue into her mouth and swallowed her answering gasp.

Unimaginable heat burst between them. Scalding. Scorching. Like falling into the sun.

Her mouth found his neck, nipping once with her teeth before climbing to suckle his bottom lip.

His moan told her how much he liked it, so she stretched the moment out a bit longer, sliding her tongue seductively along his. Lifting away, she looked into the deep brown depths of his eyes. Then she lolled her head to one side and let him explore.

His name was a sigh on her lips as his hands, his lips, his tongue slid over her, comforting and arousing all at once.

"Oh, yeah," she murmured. "Definitely have to buy Rook a huge, fat thank-you gift."

The velvet slide of his lips ended with a soft press on her temple, and his roaming hands settled on the small of her back.

A shadow of something new moved in his dark eyes. "You can't blame him for putting us together, for wanting us to find what he did." Grayson pulled her closer. "He's a man in love."

He lifted her hand from the water and placed a sweet, tender kiss in the center of her palm.

Sami's head and heart both soared. They simply lifted off and took flight, leaving her alone with this sensible and solid man. Who was talking about love.

"Don't worry, Sami. I won't stop." His thumb traced her bottom lip. "Because I can't."

Now his hands slipped along the curve of her hips to cup her backside. He held her in place as he angled one thigh between her legs.

When he moved against her, a cry tore from her lips. Pleasure coiled inside her, a hot spring twisting tighter and tighter. "Grayson." She curled her hands over his strong arms and sunk her fingers in. "I can't take it. I can't wait. I want you inside me."

Below the blue surface, she caught glimpses of lean hips and long, muscular legs. She had the urge to taste every inch of him.

But later. After the need clawing through her body found its release.

Grayson settled his hips between her thighs, and stilled, pushing the length of his erection against her most sensitive flesh. He was so hot, so close.

"Sami." As he said her name, he captured the side of her face with one hand.

She shuddered on a breath, drowning in love and lust so thick she couldn't tell where one left off and the other began.

With his smoldering eyes fastened on hers, Grayson eased his length inside of her, claiming her with his stare just as he did with his body. She wanted to keep looking at him, to stay lost in that depthless gaze, but he'd started moving inside her.

Every drop of her blood raced down and gathered, building swiftly to an unbearable ache. The coil twisted tighter, with a sweet, throbbing pull.

Then the world exploded with white-hot release. Riding crest after crest, she let her head fall back and, crying his name, she gave herself up.

~~~

Grayson saw the climax rip through Sami when her eyes closed. A ripple of tension rolled through her, leaving her long, curvy frame limp against him.

His body responded with a surge of desire, a healthy, natural yearning he'd suppressed for too long.

Here, naked and pliant in his arms, she was more beautiful than he could have imagined. And the most beautiful thing—her freely-given trust. The faith she had placed in him.

Grayson could finally face his own fear. Falling so hard, so fast for her, had left him vulnerable and uncertain. He'd always been the one to hold the cards. To decide what move came next.

But Sami kept him on his toes, always shifting and changing the playing field.

She drew a ragged breath and lifted her head, her breasts hiding just beneath the pool's surface. She met his stare, held it with her own, and tightened her legs around him.

One full, deep stroke had her clasping her arms to his neck. Another drew a whimper, and only urged him on. Holding tight, as if she'd never let go, she rose to meet his new tempo.

Leaning her against the rim of the pool, he drove deeper, darkly satisfied when her breaths started coming fast and hot. "Look at me," he demanded, pumping harder as her body tensed.

He whispered near her mouth, "Look at me," wanting to see her eyes when she peaked and they went blind with pleasure.

"Grayson, it's so much." Her pleas came in ragged gasps. "I... can't."

"Yes, you can." His hands gripped her hips as his own pistoned. "Just let go."

Her back arched like a bow. She cried out. And when she tightened around him once more, Grayson knew she was flying again.

This time, he went with her.

# 24

The blow landed hard against Sami's sword and reverberated down her arm. Panting from exertion, she wondered how many more she could fend off.

"Good job." Ronan pulled back his own weapon and reached forward to grip her shoulder for a congratulatory shake. "I think you're done."

"Thank Christmas," she said, wiping at her brow as the other trainees gathered around the practice ring applauded. Flapping her arm, numb from blocking repeated blows, she bowed to her instructor. "Just don't throw any of your explosive glass balls at me."

"No worries,' Ronan said and winked. "I'm saving all of those for Malrik's horde."

Rolling her shoulder in a circle, Sami joined her sisters among the onlookers as a young Vei Lanian male took her place in the ring. The first clang of metal on metal sent sympathy pains down her arm.

"You're getting faster," Tate said, patting Sami on the back as Fiona offered her a goblet of chilled water.

"Thanks." Sami downed the cool drink. "You guys didn't do so bad yourselves."

Fiona furrowed her brow. "I don't mind the sword, especially the smaller one Ronan suggested for me, but it still tires me too quickly."

"Any type of hand-to-hand probably won't fall to us." Tate flexed her fingers, likely sore from gripping handles and pulling bow strings. "But like Ronan said, we have to be ready for anything. What if Malrik's wizard is able to bind us somehow? What would we do if we lost access to our magick?"

"Shush." Fiona grimaced. "Losing my magick would be like losing a body part."

Sami loosed a wry chuckle. "Funny, isn't it? When barely over a year ago, we didn't even know we had any?"

A cheer rose up from the crowd, distracting Sami and her sisters. When the young blue-haired male dodged Ronan a second time, more whistles and encouragement rang out.

"Get him, kid!" Sami shouted and put her fingers in her mouth for a shrill whistle. "You get him!"

Ronan sent her a playfully disgruntled look before he performed a sort of bait-and-switch move, feinting one way but turning quickly in the other to bring his sword down sharply, stopping the point inches from the youth's chest.

More applause and cheers thundered through the air, blending with the sound of crashing surf.

Ronan helped the young man up and patted him encouragingly on the back. Then crooked his fingers in a come-at-me-again gesture.

"I'm surprised people aren't placing bets," Jack said, sidling up next to them. His blonde hair was wet with perspiration.

"Been fighting again, have you?" Tate leaned up to kiss him, then stopped, wrinkling her nose. "Maybe later. You're sweaty."

Satisfied by placing a kiss on the top of Tate's head, Jack picked a goblet of water off of a passing tray. "All we need are a few jugs of ale and this will be a party."

Sami nodded in understanding. The mood of those gathered in Vei Lani had improved over the last several days. People laughed more, they smiled more, and as evidenced by the cheering crowd, they'd developed a robust sense of camaraderie.

All in all, the general atmosphere was one of optimism.

The citizens of Vei Lani had rallied. They'd managed to produce a massive number of weapons and had honed the various skills required to use them. Sheer tenacity drove the people here, a determination to protect the lives of everyone today, as well as the way of life they hoped to pass on to future generations.

Malrik's victory could not come to pass, for it would surely result in a brutal and merciless reign of horror.

And the notion of those dark, dark times motivated everyone. A bevy of archers stood at the ready, with tens of thousands of gold-tipped arrows ready to soar.

Even the Winter Queen had gotten over her snit, lending her support, as well as hundreds of her own soldiers. Faerie and Vei Lani stood together, a formidable alliance of Fae civilizations.

And while this left the queen's castle more vulnerable to attack, all of them agreed Malrik wouldn't return to her lands.

Because he had another target in his sights.

More shouts carried from farther down the beach, so Sami stepped back to get a view of those sparring in the sand. Grayson stood off to the side, watching with his arms crossed.

As if he felt her eyes on him, he turned his head. And smiled.

Not just any smile, but one that held the secrets of the nights they'd spent entwined together. And the days working side-by-side.

With a lift of her shoulder, she sent him a flirtatious grin before glancing back to the match in front of her. But Grayson's slow smile still flashed in her mind, and a hundred butterflies set to flight in her stomach.

She placed her hand at the base of her neck, where her heart seemed to be crowding her throat. Was this love? The real-deal-once-in-a-lifetime kind of love?

Leaning back, she stole another peek at him—so serious and focused as he watched the men perform the moves he'd taught them. She had an uncontrollable urge to laugh out loud, hug herself, and spin around.

So she clamped her lips tight and settled for a secret grin.

"What are you doing?" Tate asked, though by the lift of her lips she already knew the answer.

"Just feeling energized," Sami said, which was true enough.

Standing between them, Fiona looped her arms through Sami's and Tate's. "I can feel it, too, this tingle in the air. I think it's unity." Fiona bobbed her head. "Unity and hope."

Sami not only felt it, but she saw it in the confident strides of her allies. She could hear it in their eager voices and rambunctious cheers. Hope. Fiona had nailed it. Unity and hope.

"I think we can do this," Sami said to her sisters. "No, scratch that." She turned her gaze to theirs. "We *will* do this. We're going to stop Malrik in his blood-sucking tracks."

"Stop the monster. Save the world." Tate raked her fingers through her black hair. "Sounds like an average day with the Whiteburn sisters."

Sami opened her mouth to make a pithy comeback, but shouts from a guard tower boomed from above. "Vipera! Vipera coming!"

In an instant, the crowds burst into action, everyone dispersing and heading to their assigned positions. Just like the drill they'd performed every other day.

Sami and her sisters raced toward one of the palace towers, running up the steps to the pinnacle from where they would be able to see and hear Ronan from his place in the center guard tower.

Jack and Grayson stood in the street, the main artery running from the palace and through the city toward the open valley beyond.

Rook climbed up to the tower platform and accepted a silver device from Ronan. Sami recalled the lensed apparatus, similar to binoculars.

Rook lowered the glasses and spoke aside to Ronan. Then he looked through the lenses again. "Hold!" he shouted to the archers who were already at their stations with arrows primed. "Davan rides the vipera! Hold fire!" He gave the signal for weapons down and made his way from the tower.

Ronan remained, keeping a watchful eye on the horizon.

As the sense of alarm faded to mere curiosity, Sami hurried down the steps with Tate and Fiona on her heels. They made their way out of the palace, through the courtyard, and out into the street where they went to Grayson, Jack, and Rook.

Soon Hellana appeared and, with the rest of them, waited for the dragon to land.

Sami remembered Davan to be the name of Rook's spy, and his sudden arrival didn't bode well. She wondered how he'd escaped with one of Malrik's pets, and who the other man riding on the serpent's back was.

With an unsteady thud and patter of feet, the vipera set down on the cobblestone street where people had left a clearing. "M'lord Rook," a male with black hair called out, waving his hand.

He leaped to the ground and rushed forward. "I came as fast as I could." He seemed out of breath, and slightly frantic.

Rook went to him and grabbed his hands with his own. "Davan, you're home safe." He gripped the man in a brief embrace.

"This is Tulin." Davan waved to the man still mounted on the dragon.

Then Sami looked closer. He was just a boy with huge, terrified eyes.

Davan inhaled and blew out again. "Tulin was a vipera trainer. A slave, truth be told. So he was more than happy to help me escape."

"And I brought Raynar." The young Tulin patted the vipera's head. "He's only a year old and has a sweet temperament. I couldn't let Malrik twist him into one of those monsters he rides."

Rook looked up at the boy. "You are welcome here, Tulin. You and your sweet-tempered Raynar." He smiled. "We'll have him stabled and . . . fed." Rook faltered, as if wondering exactly what vipera ate.

But he quickly turned his attention back to Davan. "Come inside, the both of you. You'll have food and drink, and then we can discuss—"

"It can't wait, m'lord." Davan shook his head. "I must tell of Malrik, of what he intends."

"Yes, we know. He's already sent raiders here, but now we're expecting a full-scale attack. And we're prepared."

Davan's features fell, his eyes full of misery. "M'lord, no. That's not what he wants. You see, he's taken magick workers, but I didn't know."

"Slow down." Rook spoke in a firm but soothing voice. "We know of Malrik's captives as well. I'm sorry you've had to endure life in that wretched place, but you're here now and you won't go back."

"I didn't know until last night, and we rode as fast as we could."

"Know what?" Rook asked.

"The Mystic, sir. Malrik has the Mystic."

Hellana gasped, as did a few other onlookers.

Rook pulled back as if he'd been struck. "Impossible. I'd gotten word the Mystic had escaped to the mountains. She's in hiding with a small contingent of her own warriors."

"It wasn't for long. Malrik got to her. He's been keeping her a secret."

"What does this mean?" Sami stepped forward. "Who is the Mystic?"

Rook lifted a hand and stared into space as if gathering his thoughts. "Every thousand years, a woman with great power is born to the Iele of Eirdorn, a distant kingdom. Her skills are . . . unrivaled."

"I listened in on Malrik's soldiers last night," Davan said. "They speak of a vast cavern and portal the Mystic created there."

"Of course!" The exclamation flew from Faidhia's crimson lips.

Sami hadn't noticed the Winter Queen's presence until she spoke.

"That explains how Malrik sent so many of his fighters to Faerie." Faidhia clasped her hands together in a ball. "Travel between our worlds is possible, but so many at once is a mighty feat."

"Malrik has his entire army ready to move," Davan reported. "They depart tomorrow eve."

"You did well," Rook told him. "Tomorrow eve, we will be ready."

"Not here, sir. The Mystic has changed the portal." Davan swallowed audibly. "He's not coming here."

"Then where?" Rook asked, gripping the spy's shoulders.

"He's planning to attack the human world," Davan said in a rush. "A land called Bar Harbor."

# 25

Sami fled the crowded street, ignoring the calls of her sisters and Grayson. Her head reeled, her eyes blurred, and all she could hear was a droning sound, like one long death knoll. A bell once rung that would never stop.

Malrik. Bar Harbor. Army.

Words batted at her as she rushed inside the palace and flew up the stairs.

Malrik was taking an army to attack Bar Harbor. An army of immortal vampires.

*And it is my fault after all.*

By the time she made it to her floor, her chest squeezed as if inside a giant vice, and her breaths expelled in painful bursts. Guilt and shame came roaring back, the knowledge that she'd doomed everyone she loved weighing on her like a mountain of stone.

*The ring. He's going for the ring.* Hadn't she known it all along? Hadn't she known she'd made a horrific mistake?

And when the tide had taken a deadly turn, where was she? Here in Vei Lani. Literally worlds away from her own home and family, who even now lay in the monster's path. Who would protect them?

Lost in her own torment, she almost ran past her room, but recognized the standing vase with a wealth of yellow blooms. She stuttered to a halt and pushed inside.

The sun hung low in the sky, casting her chamber in soft amber hues. Flinging the balcony doors open wide, she let the sea air wash over her heated face.

Another few minutes in the fresh, clean breeze, and the dense fog in her mind began to clear. Her heart no longer drummed painfully, and the clamps had stopped squeezing.

Running both hands through her hair, she dropped to a squatting position. She'd never experienced an anxiety attack before, but she'd bet money she'd just survived one.

Calmer now, Sami stayed where she was, hunched down as if hiding from fate. And as the steady wash of waves lulled and soothed, she replayed everything she'd just seen and heard.

Filing through memories like a rolodex, she pulled every important card, searching for solutions. For any way to solve the looming disaster.

Disaster? She scoffed to herself. Apocalypse seemed more fitting. Hell, they could be on the verge of human extinction.

Worrying her thumbnail, she stood and walked to the pedestal desk in one corner of the room. Paper sat neatly stacked on top, so all she needed was . . . *there*. A pen. Sort of, she thought, studying the tiny, pointed implement.

She made a few notes, a few bullets of crucial details, and was just about to sit down for further analysis when her door opened and Grayson walked in.

Facing him, she waited. Though for what she wasn't sure. What would he say? What *could* he say?

Instead, he said nothing at all. He shut the door, took a few steps closer, and simply opened his arms.

Still clenching the small pen, Sami rushed to his embrace. Sinking into his consoling warmth, she put her head on his chest, and just held on.

"I know how hard that was for you to hear." He rubbed her back in small circles.

Sniffling, and feeling like a fool, she lifted her eyes to his. "It was hard for all of us. I shouldn't have overreacted but—"

"I understand." The gentle circles continued, and his hold tightened just a bit, as if he too needed comforting.

"Of course you do." She touched his face. "Oh, God, Grayson. I'm sorry. This must be your worst nightmare. Original Iele breaking the barrier and flooding into our world."

He heaved a breath. His body went rigid. "I was a little numb at first. Shocked. Stunned. When I arrived in Maine and saw that body, the marks on the flesh only an original could make . . ." He trailed off. "This *is* my greatest fear coming true."

"I'm so sorry. I was selfish to run away."

"I went to my own dark corner," he said. "I think we all did." He lifted a shoulder, still touching her, still soothing. "Maybe it's just who I am. Maybe it's a lifetime of control and training. Or maybe, it's knowing my men and I are no longer alone."

His voice softened, yet held conviction. "But I'm not giving up. I can't. This is the crisis we have to deal with, so that's what I'll do. What we'll all do. Together."

"I can't believe I'm saying this," she said, burrowing in, "but thank the gods for your logical, practical mind."

When he gave her a squeeze, she looked up. "We have to reorient," he said, "but consider what we still have. The army we've built may be here, but the roots of my organization run deep. We have options, and we have backup."

"Yes," Sami said. "I've been doing exactly that. Considering." She blew out through pursed lips. "After I recovered from my meltdown."

His laughter was a low rumble in his chest. "I think you're entitled to one. You might have buried your guilt, maybe even beaten it, but regret can leave ghosts behind. Ugly echoes to rise up when you least expect it."

She thought of the night that had altered his life, of the guilt he'd carried himself for so long. "You do understand." And yet, after what they'd just learned and as hard as this had to be for him, he'd come to bring her solace.

She wiped at the tears that had sprung out of nowhere. "Thank you. I guess I needed to talk. I needed you."

He pressed a kiss to her forehead. "I did, too," he said and began to pull away.

"Wait." She clung to him, afraid to let him go just yet. "Can you hold me? Just a little longer?"

When he grinned and dragged her back in, she hid her face in his shoulder. "I must seem pretty weak."

Not roughly, but not gently either, he lifted her chin and forced her to meet his gaze. "How can you say that?" He shook his head. "Sami, you are one of the strongest women—one of the strongest *people* I know. After what we've come to mean to each other, I'd hope you would lean on me. I'd hope you'd know that you can."

"I do." She snuggled in, greedy for the security, for the safety his touch provided. For several minutes, they stood like that in silence with the occasional caress.

The longer Sami stayed pressed against him, the closer she longed to be. "Grayson?" Her voice sounded small to her own ears.

"Hmm?" He kissed the top of her head.

Just as Jack had done to Tate earlier. Such a casual gesture, a sign of endearment.

Shifting in his arms, Sami leaned into him, twirling her fingers in the center of his chest. "I want to be with you."

He raised a solitary brow, and for a moment she feared he wouldn't respond. Then he asked, "You want me to make love to you?"

She shrugged. "I said be with."

He lowered his mouth for a lingering kiss. Then he stared deeply into her eyes. "And I said *love*."

Sami's heart leaped up. It filled her body, and she suddenly felt as if liquid gold coursed in her veins—warm, thick, and rich. Yet the warmth stemmed from something far more valuable than precious metals or jewels.

"Love," she whispered to him. And it was all she had to say.

As Grayson grinned like the cat who'd gotten his canary, Sami angled her head to shoot him a sidelong glance. "I knew from the start you were a sneaky bastard."

"Yeah, well, this kind of snuck up on me, too." He trailed a finger down her cheek. "I've lost a certain amount of control where you're concerned, but I wouldn't change it, even if I could."

"Because we've changed each other. How we see things, how we see ourselves." She sighed. "I didn't want to trust you. I didn't want to need you. But I do."

As the situation they faced returned front and center to her mind, she gripped his hands. "And it can't all be for nothing, Grayson. I want more time with you. I want a future. I want to see where we—"

"Shhh." When panic made a bid for escape, he tapped her lips. "Easy, baby. Easy." The sturdy and rational man she knew him to be made an appearance. "So we got bad news. I reeled and recovered, and you've beaten yourself up all over again. We've both cycled through and have come back around to the central question. What next?"

He glanced over her head. "I saw you working at the desk over there, so don't tell me your wheels aren't churning."

"Yes, they are." She blew out long and hard. "The news from Rook's spy is bad, like a horse kick straight to the head." And to the gut, the heart, the soul.

"So now what?" he prodded.

"We certainly can't just lie down and die." She clenched her jaw. "And I'm sure as hell not giving up on my hometown and my friends and family. Not to mention the innocent people living in Bar Harbor, all of Mount Desert Island, and beyond. Because what you said before is true. Malrik is power hungry, and he won't stop there."

"No, he won't. So it's still up to us. We still have to be the ones who stop him."

"After I got through beating myself up," she hip-bumped him and grinned, "I started thinking, lining things up, all the players and the moving pieces."

"You're good at that, taking the parts and rearranging them. Visualizing the whole."

"Seeing the big picture," she said, thinking back to the day in her barn, in her workshop, where he'd first told her what he saw.

What he saw in her.

"Okay, so tell me. What's in the picture?"

After a pause, she said, "Possibilities."

"Then let's lay it out. We'll strategize together, and then we'll go to the others."

"Oh, uh . . . not just yet." Standing on her toes, she looped her arms around his neck. "We can spare a few more minutes, and I always think better when I'm nice and relaxed. And right now, I think we should both relax and re-center. We've got a lot of work ahead of us, and I'm going to take this moment with you while I can."

She tugged him toward her bed. "Grayson, I need you to *make love* to me." She tossed his words back at him. "And I have to say, I've gotten used to having you by my side."

Without protest, Grayson followed. He laid her down. "No matter what happens, whatever we face, that's exactly where I intend to stay."

"Good." Running her hands up under his shirt, she melted into the soft covers. "That's good, because after this, we can work on strategy." When his lips descended to hers, she whispered, "Because I think I have a plan."

# 26

The return trip through the portal had been far less unnerving, since this time Grayson knew what to expect. Still, traveling from the Ielonaar Realm to the human world in a matter of steps mixed up his sense of time and space.

With the sun only an orange memory toward the West, he followed Sami across the lawn of the Whiteburn property and up to the side door of the huge white house. They slipped inside to find her grandfather the sole occupant of the kitchen.

"You're back," he said, leaping from his seat at the long wooden table to rush to Sami, enveloping her in a hug before reaching around her to shake Grayson's hand.

Studying the agile man with silver hair, Grayson gestured to the cane he was never without. "Tell me, Niall. You always have that cane but never need it. Why do you carry it?"

"For Fae intruders, of course." In two quick steps, her grandfather seized the cane and removed what turned out to be only a wooden sheath. Concealing the long, sharp sword inside. He held up the tip for Grayson's inspection. "Sami added the gold for me in the spring, when our Iele presence suddenly increased."

"Nice," Grayson said, and meant it. He might broach the idea of having Sami make one for his own grandfather. But at a later time, after the current infestation had been dealt with.

"Nadia! Brit!" Niall called out for Sami's mother and uncle, both of whom hurried into the kitchen.

At the same time, Tate and Fiona entered from the side yard to an exchange of hugs and greetings.

"Where are Jack and Ronan?" Brit asked, staring at the open door.

"Outside," Sami said, "with our guests. I just wanted to prepare you first." She went to the door and said, "Come on in."

Arelia, the voice of reason from the Vei Lanian council, stepped inside with hands folded and her smile wide. "Hello, and thank you for welcoming me into your home." She moved to stand with Fiona as two Vei Lanian males trailed in after her.

Arelia, it turned out, possessed certain gifts of her own, as did the men, Dar and Stefin. And if Sami's idea went as planned, the powers of all three would be put to use.

And that plan, Grayson thought as he crossed his arms to watch, included one more important person.

Still near the door, Sami dropped her shoulders and exhaled. "And this," she gestured, palm extended and expression flat, " is Faidhia. The Winter Queen."

Faidhia sauntered in, sparing Sami a disgusted look. "If that's your idea of how royalty should be announced . . ." She turned to the group and rolled her shoulders.

Sniffing and ignoring the shock on Brit's face, the queen made a beeline for Sami's mother with a flourish of hands. "I finally make the acquaintance of the famous and prophesied Nadia. Such an honor." Her crimson smile stood out against milky skin. "The famous Nadia," she repeated, "who managed to beget three of the most irritating creatures in all the worlds."

Sami's mother only laughed and bowed her head. "You are most welcome here, Your Highness, and I'm sorry for the . . . difficulties between you and my daughters."

Faidhia nodded obligingly. "I believe I can let bygones be bygones." She glared at Tate. "*If* this scheme is successful." She eased away from Sami's mother and took up a position next to

Arelia as Jack and Ronan joined the crowd in the kitchen.

"Is Kat awake?" Tate asked Brit, getting down to business. "Did she get Rook's message?"

"Yes." Brit's mouth flattened into worried lines. "A horrible thing to learn from a bowl of water. That a horde of vampire soldiers might be showing up in our back yard."

"I hope it didn't upset Kat," Fiona said. "But we had to—"

"No. No." Brit shook his head. "She's fine, and we all get it. Lives are at stake. The whole damn world." He shoved his hands in the pocket of his jeans.

Grayson could see the fears of a man about to become a father. But when sympathy and apprehension arose, he had to balance them with the main goal. He had millions of fathers to think about now, and he couldn't get sidetracked by this new association, or his fondness for the Whiteburn clan.

Sami had been right. This was Grayson's worst nightmare. But if this plan worked . . .

"Brit and I prepared the items you asked for." Sami's mother opened a drawer and retrieved a sheet of paper and a glass vial of ink.

Sami had explained this concept to him. Specter paper and beetle ink. Now he was about to see the magick for himself.

Tate took the paper and gripped the lid of the small bottle.

"Wait." Sami touched Tate's arm. "Should we create the map if what we're looking for isn't here yet? Will it even work?"

Tate frowned. "I didn't think of that. Damn. But how will we know when Malrik and his troops arrive? We have no idea where they'll enter this world. Main Street? The harbor? The other side of the island?" She threw up her hands. "How can we even guess?"

"We don't have to guess." Kat stood in the doorway, skin pale and eyes terrified. "I can feel the change. It's happening now."

"Yes." Arelia moved to the bay window overlooking the front yard. She lifted her arm straight out, and pointed. "There."

A concussive blast erupted from the direction she'd indicated, rolling across the island like thunder from the gods. A flash of light—white and short-lived—lit up the sky.

"Eagle Lake," Kat whispered, pressing a hand to her belly, to the precious life within. "They're coming now."

A stunned silence reigned over those gathered.

Until Grayson moved to Sami's side, glanced to the paper on the kitchen table, and said, "It's time to make that map."

~~~

Keeping to the cover of the nighttime forest, Sami crept along the edge of the lake. "Up there," she said, gesturing to the spread of exposed rock. Huge swaths of stone covered the hillside, having erupted from beneath the ground in millennia past.

And milling on the rocks, covering the rugged incline like a swarm, was Malrik's army.

"There are so many," Sami whispered, her gut lurching. Knowing they were coming was one thing. Seeing hundreds of brutish blood-drinking monsters only miles outside of town?

A vastly different level of terror.

"We all know what we're supposed to do." This from Ronan who'd come to crouch beside her and Grayson. Tate, Fiona, Jack, and Brit hung farther back. Along with the Winter Queen, who'd been none too happy about hiking over the "savage human landscape," as she'd put it.

Sami and Grayson nodded, and then Sami waved Brit closer. "Take the others and wait for us at the Jordan Pond trail."

"That's the best spot," Brit agreed. "Limited sight because of the trees lining the trail, and the open path will steer them all in the right direction."

"They won't bottleneck," Grayson added, "but they'll go where we want them to."

"Exactly." Sami nodded in the dark. "At least, we hope they will."

"Stay positive," Ronan said. "This will work, Sami. It's a good plan. We just have to make it work."

"Like clockwork," Sami murmured, anxiety spreading outward from her center. She took a calming breath and let the tension release. "Okay, we'll meet you there."

Brit and Ronan left to inform the others, while Sami and Grayson waited for Faidhia. When the imperious Fae woman sidled closer, Sami pointed out the army of vampires again. "How close do you need to get?"

Faidhia narrowed her eyes. "The bottom of the rise should work. I'll wait until you return."

"Let's move," Grayson told them, holding his hand out to escort the queen through the shadowed forest.

"Don't get any ideas, Faidhia." Sami hiked a warning brow.

"Don't be silly." The queen actually giggled. "You know my heart belongs to Jack."

Surprised to find herself smiling, Sami led Grayson and the queen to the area Faidhia had suggested. "I'm ready," the queen said instantly.

"Okay." Grayson put a hand to the dagger at his hip. "Sami, the map."

She pulled the folded paper from her pocket, opened the parchment she and her sisters had doused with beetle ink, and waited for the little blue beetle to flash and walk in the direction she and Grayson should follow.

Grayson leaned in. And jerked his head when the tiny bug appeared to walk across the paper.

Unlike the night another beetle had led Sami and her sisters to the underground tunnels, this insect made no twists or turns. Instead, he marched across the paper in a straight path, the blue dotted lines behind it changing to brown.

"X marks the spot?" Grayson asked.

"Yes. That's where we'll find what we're looking for." Sami held the map out for guidance. If they stepped off course, the map would let them know.

Faidhia lifted her chin. She closed her eyes. "Go now."

A prickling wave rolled over Sami, and judging by Grayson's reaction, he'd felt it, too. "She's doing it?" he asked. "Casting the illusion?"

"Yes." Sami notched her chin and exited the forest. "We're covered, but we need to do this fast." Wasting no time, she began a cautious but swift climb up the hill, toward the rocky outcropping.

And straight toward the pack of murderous warriors.

Beside her, Grayson never faltered, he never slowed. His faith in magick allowing him to walk into the mass of vampires.

Sami forced herself to breathe evenly, keeping her eyes on the map. "Almost there," she said.

Grayson looked at her. "They can't hear us either?"

"No. Not as long as Faidhia's illusion holds." The Winter Queen had cast a net of Fae magick, one that kept Sami and Grayson concealed from the Iele.

Three fiends abruptly crossed in front of them. Sami and Grayson both halted. And tensed.

The near-miss left Sami's heart thumping against her ribs, but they continued on, following the lines on the paper created by the beetle.

"There she is," Sami said, gesturing to an old woman in a navy-blue mantle. "The X is there," she whispered with excitement. "That's the Mystic."

They continued to advance, and Sami saw the moment the Mystic realized they were coming to her.

Quizzical wrinkles creased her forehead. "Who are you? Human?" She glanced around with wide eyes. "You shouldn't be here."

"It's safe," Sami assured her. "You don't know us, and we don't have long to explain. But we need you to come with us."

"What? No. I—"

"We need your help," Grayson told her. "We can stop Malrik, but not without you."

"We are covered by an illusion now, and so are you." Sami held out her hands in entreaty. "The Winter Queen is here. She and others who've been hurt by Malrik."

"Why do you need me? What do you have planned?" She swatted the air and shook her head. "No. No. This is madness." Again, her gaze darted to the fanged beasts looming on all sides. "I can't go with you. I can't help you. I won't take that risk."

"You're afraid of what they'll do to your granddaughter," Grayson stated plainly.

The Mystic froze, her mouth falling open. "How do you know of her?"

"We know everything, and we can bring Malrik's rampage to an end," Sami insisted. "But only with your help."

"I'm sorry." Now the woman's eyes filled with sorrow. "It's too dangerous. I can't make a move against him. Not as long as he has my granddaughter."

Sami took the old woman's hands in her own, leaned closer, and said, "About that."

# 27

Hellana and Rook burst free of the water and surveyed the dark, dank surroundings. "This is the place," Rook said, just as four more Vei Lanian men surfaced from the underground spring. Two of them were water-drifts with the ability to travel as Rook did, and the other two their passengers.

The additional men had been brought by the water-drifts for the purpose of the mission, both strong soldiers, able to fight.

Hellana scanned the dirty walls and slime-covered floors. "This is the natural waterway running beneath the tombs." Based on the information Davan had gathered for Rook, they'd pinpointed this area as their destination.

And now that she was here, in Malrik's kingdom, childhood memories flashed behind her eyes. "I used to play here," she said, wading to the edge to climb out. "Hiding really." She made a derisive sound in her throat. "Imagine a home life so bad that a little girl prefers to stay in decrepit old tombs."

"We don't have to stay long." Rook exited the water and gripped her shoulders. "You can wait here if you want."

The offer warmed Hellana, because it was so like him to think of her first. Even now. But no matter Rook's affection for her, or his concern, she'd come to help. "No, no. If we are captured, my status as Malrik's daughter might—*might* buy us some mercy." She pictured Malrik's guards, all vicious, lecherous beasts. "But don't count on it."

Despite the filthy water still dripping from her face, Rook pulled her in and kissed her lips. "Where you lead, I shall follow. My queen," he added, the light in his gaze reflecting more than friendly interest.

And to her continued surprise, Hellana returned the sentiment. "Let's win this day, Rook." She returned the kiss. And she stretched hers out just a little bit longer. "Then we'll see. About everything."

"As you wish, m'lady." Smiling, he led her and the other men down the central corridor, following the underground stream to the center of the tombs. Once there, he pointed to another hallway, one lined with wooden doors. Locked from the outside.

"It seems clear. Quiet," one of the water-drifts said.

"That's what makes me nervous." Hellana looked around before walking down the passage. They'd expected most of Malrik's men to be gone, but still, the task warranted caution.

"Get those doors open." Rook directed the four men to start cutting locks with the tools they'd brought. Though they tried to do so quietly, the clank of metal against metal echoed through the halls like broken bells.

"Who goes there?" A hulking silhouette filled the far end of the corridor. And was instantly joined by another.

"Rook," Hellana said.

"I see them. Just keep working on the locks."

The two brawlers who'd come along marched toward the guards, each brandishing their weapons.

Hellana broke a lock and opened the door. "Come. Hurry." She waved a frantic hand at the two prisoners inside. "You're free," she told a man. "Go down this way, follow the water out of the tombs. Make your way to Grogin's pass. Do you know it?"

When he nodded, she continued. "People will come for you, Vei Lanians. Just wait for them there."

"May the gods bless you, my lady." He scrambled away with the other man who'd shared his cell.

She glanced to Rook and saw him escorting a very old woman with a small child. Repeating Hellana's words, he gave them the same instructions.

Sounds of fighting had filled the tight space, but now they dissipated. Rook's men returned from the short conflict and began breaking locks again.

Rook opened two more doors. Hellana another. Still nothing.

"Rook, where?" Panic crawled along her skin. "I thought Davan said—"

"He did. Just keep searching."

Hellana struggled against the fear. Every step was crucial. They couldn't fail.

Fighting apprehension, she raised the hammer to smash another lock, when one of the water-drifts called, "Rook!"

Hellana whirled to find the man lifting one arm. "Here! She's here!"

~~~

"Are you sure my granddaughter is safe?" The Mystic crept over the jagged rocks with Sami.

Relieved to get away from the army without detection, Sami guided the older woman with caution. "We'll know shortly," she assured her. "Look, there they are."

Still trying to maintain stealth, Sami and Grayson increased their pace but kept their steps light. They met up with the rest of the group. Which had grown by two more members.

"Finley." Grayson gave his friend a one-armed man-hug before turning to do the same to Dodge. "It is damn good to see you guys."

"You know we got you covered, brother." Dodge slapped Grayson's butt. "We called in a few more teams after you left to . . . the Iele Realm."

"Close enough," Sami said and grinned.

"What of my granddaughter?" The Mystic broke into the conversation. "I must return or Malrik—"

"Your granddaughter is safe. She is in the kingdom of Vei Lani."

The old woman swooned, clapping a hand to her chest and closing her eyes. "Thank the gods." Her eyes opened. "And thank all of you, whoever you are. How can you be certain?" she asked Brit.

"Our friend Rook has your granddaughter with him, and he sent word to my wife." Brit held up his cell phone. "And she just called to relay the good news."

"Oh, thank you. *Thank you.*" The Mystic moved amongst them, touching shoulders or hands as she did. Her gratitude and obvious love for her granddaughter brought a sting to Sami's eyes.

Even the sober Winter Queen broke a smile.

Once she'd thanked them all, the Mystic straightened her spine and faced Sami. "Now. How shall I be of service? I long to have my vengeance on Malrik and his revolting breed."

They explained what they needed the Mystic to do. After she'd asked all of her questions, she wrung her hands. "I can do it. Yes. I'm certain I can."

She studied the eclectic gathering, pointing to Brit, Tate, and Fiona. "I'll need your help. I'll need a boost."

"Anything you need," Tate said, "we'll make it happen."

Her promise still hung in the air when a great gust of wind raked across Eagle Lake, blowing in from the direction of the Atlantic Ocean. Clouds, dark as midnight and roiling like a witch's brew, rushed across the night sky. They were only visible due to the bolts of white lightning flashing from within.

"Looks like Mom, Granddad, and the Vei Lanians are doing their part." Fiona held out her hand to catch rain as it pelted down. "Arelia said she and her friends could call a storm."

"But this is the storm to end them all," Jack said.

"Or one to save the world." Ronan kissed Fiona's temple.

"What is this?" the Mystic asked.

"Our backup plan," Grayson told her. "In the event what we're about to try fails. We needed the storm. We needed a tempest." He eyed the frightening skies. "To keep people safely inside."

In case vampires started roaming the streets in search of prey.

"Dodge and I will be in the forest with the teams." Finley glanced to the tall trees. "To catch any of those bastards that slip free or make a run for it."

"Then everything's in place." Sami reached out and gripped Grayson's hand. "We're all set."

Drawing a breath, she slid her hand into her pocket. "Only one more step." And likely the most crucial part of her plan.

She started to turn away, to leave and do her part, but instinct had her waiting. Just long enough to look at her sisters, Brit, and all the men who'd joined her family since that first night, that first quest, when three sisters went in search of a mysterious key.

"I love you. I love you all."

Tate and Fiona broke from the line and ran to her. She was wrapped up in their arms, squeezing tight, when Brit came over and embraced all three in one big rain-soaked hug.

Only seconds passed, but in that brief, sweet moment, Sami recalled a lifetime of shared memories—love, joy, sadness, loss, triumph. And through it all, the flow of magick, even when they hadn't known it was there.

"You'll be okay," Tate insisted. "It's going to work."

"Damn straight," Fiona added. "And we'll be ready. We'll be waiting." Her eyes watered. "You won't be alone for long, Sami."

"I know it." She patted Fiona's face and winked at Tate and Brit. "I need to go."

But before she did, one more thing. She stepped to Grayson, curled her fingers into his shirt, and pulled him to her. "I love you, LeRoux. And don't you ever forget it."

"Not a chance in hell." He lowered his lips to hers for a tender kiss. "I'll see you soon, and you can remind me just how much. Hey, Sami." He grabbed her elbow when she made a move to go. "Don't you forget." He gave her that wicked grin. "I love you, too."

With the thrill from his words still rocking through her system, she took another deep breath for courage, walking backwards. She retreated in the direction of the rock-covered hills. "I'll give you three minutes," she called through the pounding rain.

The Mystic nodded. "Plenty of time."

Hand still in her pocket, Sami trudged over wet grass and pockets of mud, making the climb up the hill to the swarming vampires. Counting off in her head, she made sure she took enough time.

And hoped it had been enough when the first soldiers spotted her.

"My name is Sami Whiteburn, and I've come for Malrik." Lightning streaked and thunder boomed, while rain streamed from merciless skies. She pulled her hand from her pocket, and with it, the ring.

Slipping the gemstone on her finger, she raised her fist in challenge. "Tell him I have something he wants."

~~~

Malrik pushed through his troops, elbowing the slower ones out of his way. His men had come to him, ranting about a woman. A crazy human who had his ring.

Shoving to the front of the pack, he stared down at the foolish woman with long wet hair. What was she doing? Did she think she could beat him?

He didn't spend long wondering over her motives, and she shouted at him from below. "Here is the ring, Malrik!" She shook her fist, the long-coveted green stone flashing with each burst of lightning.

"Bring me what is mine, witch!" He extended his arm, held out his palm. "Bring it to me now, and I will spare your life."

"I will never give you the ring." She cackled then, turning her face up to the storm. "The power is mine. All mine." She curled her hand to her chest. "I'm taking the stone away from here, away from you and all of your filth."

She rushed forward a few steps. "I'm too strong for you, Malrik. I beat the men you sent here, and that was before I tasted the power for myself. Now you will never defeat me."

She edged back, a hateful smile spreading over her face. "Bring your soldiers, bring your flying beasts. But you will never find me!"

Spinning on her heels, the mad witch raced into the dark.

Astonished by her temerity, insulted by her claims, Malrik clenched his fists and pounded them on his chest. "Ready my mount! Call up the men!" Rage set fire to his brain and turned his vision red.

Starting down the hill, he continued to shout orders. "All infantry, all riders!" He circled his arm forward with a jerk. "Get me that ring!"

War cries from his army resounded through the night, loud enough to rival the drilling rain. Still following the witch toward the forest, he raked his tongue over the tips of his fangs. Tonight, he would have the ring. Tonight, he would wield the power.

And tonight, he would drink his fill—from the human witch who'd cost him so much.

Swords clattered and boots tromped as hundreds of vampires gave chase. Even as he strode boldly to the woods, his army poured down the hills around him.

"There! She's taken a turn down that path!" Spying the witch, Malrik walked faster.

Even as his soldiers raced ahead of him, the flap of vipera wings rumbled from the sky.

"Here, sire." A mounted rider landed nearby on Malrik's most-trusted creature. As his man jumped down, Malrik climbed onto the dragon's back. On his command, Fulgar flew.

In eager pursuit, Malrik leaned forward, pushing the vipera to its limits. He spotted the narrow trail the witch had taken and dug his heels into Fulgar's sides.

Soaring down the narrow path, Malrik searched for the duplicitous witch. The pass was shrouded in darkness, but he was certain she'd come this way.

Around him, his army rushed—some ahead, some falling behind—as the forest closed in on both sides.

*Where is she? Where is that bitch of a human?* Malrik soared onward. "I want that ring!" he shouted as he whipped along the trail.

He had to be gaining on her. She'd been on foot.

Another blast of lightning and thunder exploded together, and as Malrik shielded his eyes, the blackness faded. The sky began to change.

Where once there had been storm clouds and rain, now there was a sharp, brilliant blue, and the midday sun.

"What sorcery is this?" Slowing his mount, he whipped his head around to survey the terrain. Mountains rose on either side with a boulder-strewn valley in between. Confused and furious, he landed Fulgar and quickly dismounted.

Whirling, he tried to make sense of the new surroundings. Then helplessly, he turned, watching the rest of his army filter through. All of them having fallen for the same trap.

As he spun in circles, staring at the strange lands, he heard a voice call from above.

"Welcome home, Malrik." The witch stood on an outcropping of rock, waving her hand. And still wearing his ring.

Threats and curses rose to his lips, but they all died when others began to reveal themselves. Vei Lanians, by the look of them.

Soldiers, warriors mounted on four-legged steeds, and rows of archers high in the hills.

With arrows notched.

Malrik's head tightened. His chest ached with rage. His mind raced for answers, but none could be found.

He didn't know how. He didn't know why. But somewhere, somehow . . . he'd traveled back to the Ielonaar Realm.

# 28

Muscles coiled, ready to leap, Grayson stood ready with Sami's dagger in his right hand and a Vei Lanian blade in the other. He found the shorter, curved swords to his liking, able to fend off a blow from a distance, or sweep up under an opponent for a belly-cut.

Like him, the Vei Lanians held fast, poised to engage. The time hadn't come, but had to be only seconds away.

"Wait. Not yet." Ronan held his hand up, one finger raised. "Not yet."

"The last of the vipera have made it through the portal." The Mystic spoke from where she stood next to Sami, behind Ronan.

Grayson peered around to meet her gaze. "How can you be sure?"

"Young man," she tossed her mantle off of her shoulders, "I am the Mystic."

Since that was apparently the only answer he'd be getting—and because it had been delivered with such aplomb—Grayson sent the older woman a cheeky grin, before returning his attention to the battle at hand.

"I need to close the portal." The Mystic closed her eyes.

"Just a little longer," Ronan argued. "We need to get as many through as possible."

With a huff, the Mystic relented.

And just as quickly, Ronan chin-notched toward Malrik. "He's seen his only option. He's about to issue the command. Now," he added, turning sharply to the Mystic. "Do it now."

"It's practically done." With an expression of a yogi in meditation, the woman stood stock still. Then a thunderous *boom!* ricocheted through the valley, accompanied by a quick flash of light.

Still holding up one hand, Ronan said, "Some of Malrik's soldiers may have been left behind."

"That's okay." Grayson clenched and relaxed his fingers on the dagger's hilt. "Finley and Dodge will be there with the teams. They'll take care of any stragglers."

"Good. Get ready." Ronan looked back to Sami, Tate and Jack, and of course, his Fiona. He tossed her a wink, nodded to Brit, and lowered his arm. "Attack!" He made a cutting motion then, his straight hand shooting forward.

The first volley of arrows flew, striking the monsters still huddled in confused disarray below. Any monster was fair game, vipera and vampire alike.

Shouts and roars spewed forth, with some fiends running and others dropping to writhe on the ground. Malrik was the first to kick his dragon and hurtle up into the sky, while his commanding officers frantically tried to make order from chaos.

Grayson itched to get down there among the vampires, to do what he did best. Send demons back to Hell.

Across the valley, another line of archers prepared to loose their arrows. And did so in answer to Rook's call of "Fire!"

In anticipation, Grayson moved closer to the edge. He glanced over to see Sami doing the same, along with a line of her family. Brit had his favored weapon in hand and was already shooting bolts from his ancient bow. Jack gripped his axes in both hands, with a bevy of knives and other sharp objects tucked away and ready to be thrown with deadly accuracy.

Ronan commanded troops on this side of the valley, but he too had a sword at the ready.

And the Whiteburn women? Well, they stood there like three ladies just waiting for their turn to dance. Three beautiful ladies, each with fire in their palms and expressions of lethal intent.

"Malrik comes!" the Mystic shouted, her eyes hard on the sky as a vipera dove toward the ridge.

Sami and Tate both flung fire, but Malrik's beast swerved, evading their white flames as the dragon's shadow covered them all.

"Now, Ronan." Grayson put a foot forward.

"Yes," Ronan pulled the long blade from across his back, "I think you're right." With a war cry to send shivers down any creature's spine, Ronan held his sword aloft, and charged. The Vei Lanian troops followed, and the archers sent their last unified volley. With the battle raging, they would now change tactics, choosing targets individually and aiming for their hearts.

The sun shone bright above as Grayson and the others sprinted downhill, no glare to blind them as they made their assault, other than when they looked up. To a sky filled with circling dragons.

Near him, Sami released her magick, scorching fiends both left and right. She and her sisters went first to their fire, controlling the bursts to avoid burning an ally.

A vampire lunged at Grayson, so he dipped low and stabbed high. When the creature fell, he sliced him again across the throat, then left him to shrivel away as he died. More came at him, a never-ending barrage. But the moves he'd learned so long ago served him, and saved him, as the lightning-fast brutes charged from all sides.

Over the clash of swords and the screams of death, Malrik's voice rang out. "Ogin!" he cried, diving toward the ground. "Ogin! Find the witches! Take them out!"

Distracted for the briefest moment, Grayson felt a slash on his arm. Falling into his rhythm once again, he focused on the fight and shouted to Sami. "Did you hear that?"

"I heard it. I—" Sami's back arched and her face clenched as if she were in great pain.

"Sami!" Still on the offensive, Grayson spun and crouched, moving to her as fast as he could to stand over her body. "What is it? Are you hurt?"

Terror was a stab to his soul. "Sami, what is it?" *Control your emotions.*

She was so vulnerable down there. *Don't get distracted.*

Jack and Ronan roared . . . as Tate and Fiona fell. *Focus over feelings.*

Pulling from a place deep inside, Grayson swung the blades in his hands like a madman. He didn't know how to help Sami, but he'd damn well stand guard. For her, for their love, his emotions didn't distract. They *motivated.*

"Magick." Still grimacing, she spit out the word a second time. "Magick. The wizard. Binding us."

Magick. In his chest, Grayson's heart turned to stone. He couldn't fight magick. He didn't know how.

But others did.

"Mystic!" he yelled, praying she would hear him, or sense him, as he continued to block the attacks of the surrounding horde. "Mystic! The wizard!" *Please, hear me.*

Soon he heard Brit shouting for the older woman as well.

And a strange golden light spread across the valley like a detonation.

Twisting, Grayson searched for her, for the Mystic. He found her gliding—floating—down the mountain and across the craggy landscape. In his mind, he would swear he heard her say, *Keep fighting, young man. I've got this one.*

A dark cloud passed close by. No, it was Malrik again, still soaring high above, unwilling to fight for himself.

"Sami, hold on." The attacks from Malrik's men seemed to be lessening, though not enough for him to grow careless. And as long as she was lying down there, in agony, Grayson would be up here, slicing away.

A horrific, high-pitched scream streaked through the valley. Immediately after, Malrik bellowed his rage.

And Sami's body relaxed. Blinking, she stared up at Grayson. "You took care of me," she said, as if still in a daze.

"Just take your time, because I've got you." He swung up and decapitated a charging vamp. "I've got you."

Another moment, and she seemed to get her bearings. The mass of bodies had begun to thin, with far more Vei Lanians standing than the black-and-red-armored enemy troops.

Sami gained her feet and resumed firing, easing closer to Grayson to battle back-to-back.

As they fought together, a vipera shrieked overhead. A spear of ice jutted from its side.

"That's the Winter Queen," Sami said and laughed. "By the gods, Grayson," she actually took the time to bump her butt to his, "I think we're winning."

~ ~ ~

Finally allowing herself to grow hopeful again, Sami blasted at vampires like a kid playing whack-a-mole. She could sense the proverbial tide turning, and it turned in favor of the good guys.

"Sami!"

She thought she heard her voice in the wind.

"Tate! Fiona!"

There it was again, only not her name.

"Do you hear that?" she asked Grayson, charring a vipera's belly when it dove toward Brit and Ronan.

Spinning, but still attacking, Sami searched the battlefield. Bodies lay piled atop each other, but most of them were the dry husks of dead vampires.

"Sami!" This time, she tracked the cry, and saw Hellana and Rook fighting their way through the remaining throng.

"Grayson." She jerked her head. "Something's up."

"Stick by me," he said. "We'll get closer." He jumped back, just in time, avoiding a vipera as it crash-landed. "We're gaining. No question about it. We just have to keep it up a little longer."

Searching for her sisters, Sami found them standing together with Jack and Ronan on their outer flanks. Brit was behind them, shooting bolts at the mounted riders.

He'd balk if anyone accused him of being kind-hearted, but he was only shooting at the soldiers, as if he hoped the dragons would simply flee.

"Brit," Sami called out, no longer having to shout. The din of combat had lessened. "Rook and Hellana," she said by way of explanation, gesturing to the blue-haired couple as they approached, leaping over and evading corpses.

Rook shouted something that sounded like "Aaargh," and then started pointing wildly toward a large boulder. The stone mass stood at least twenty feet high, but she couldn't understand what he was trying to tell them.

Rook and Hellana finally made it to where she and Grayson stood. Soon her sisters arrived, with Brit, Jack, and Ronan crowding around. Jack and Ronan continued to fend off the occasional assault, though they were fewer and fewer.

"There, behind the stone." Rook took a moment to catch his breath. "They're coming."

Examining the massive boulder again, Sami squinted, and at last understood. Three figures in gray-hooded robes strode slowly out from behind the promontory. As if carbon copies of one another, they walked in sync, hands hanging at their sides.

"Who is that?" Fiona asked, crinkling her forehead as she stared.

"The spellcasters taken captive from Faerie," Hellana said.

"They are the Skaar," Rook added, "and they are death on the wind."

"The war is practically over." Sami gestured to the valley and the remaining Vei Lanians. The victors.

"But not over yet." Rook gazed skyward. Malrik still lives, and while he does, the family members of his captives may still be in danger."

"You and Hellana set them free," Sami said. "You released them."

"Yes." Rook sent a fearful look to the approaching Skaar. "But they don't know that."

"So we'll just tell them." Fiona stepped forward, but Sami put out a halting hand. "Sure, Fee. We'll do that. But we means *we*." Trailing a hand down Grayson's uninjured arm, Sami told him, "Let us handle this."

She could tell he didn't care for the idea, but Rook had described the Skaar as spellcasters. And just like sword met sword, and fist punched flesh . . . magick spoke to magick.

Silently, Sami and her sisters fell into a line, and together they went to meet the Skaar.

"What exactly do spellcasters do?" Fiona asked.

Tate shook her head. "I'm afraid we're about to find out."

"I'll try telepathy." Sami made the announcement before concentrating on sending her voice to the three solemn figures gradually coming closer. *You don't have to fight. Your families are safe now.*

The Skaar gave no indication that they'd heard her, and they showed no signs of stopping.

"Try yelling," Tate said through clenched teeth. "I'm getting a bad vibe."

"So am I," Fiona whispered.

"You don't have to do this!" Sami yelled.

At once, and in unison, the Skaar halted. Movement coordinated as if they'd practiced, the three spellcasters raised their arms and pushed back their hoods. Each had a shock of white hair atop their heads, cut short in identical styles.

Sami stopped walking, too. "What. The. Hell."

When she felt the vibration, she automatically glanced to the ground. "Tate. Fee."

"I feel it." Fiona spread out her hands as if to balance.

"It's them," Tate said with certainty. "It's the Skaar."

"And they're just getting started." Sami jogged forward. "Wait!"

But the Skaar had already sent out a blast of magick, and it rolled across the ground scattering rocks into the air as it passed.

Instinctively, Sami held out her hands and pushed. She didn't think, and she didn't plan. She only reacted, imagining her power as a solid wave rising up to block the Skaar's strike.

When her power met theirs, she stumbled back. Then Tate and Fiona stepped up, throwing their own surge toward the spellcasters. This time, the Skaar lost their balance, and Sami took the opportunity to shout, "Your families are safe. They've been set free!"

Did they hesitate? She thought maybe—

As one, they turned palms to the sky, and a shrill ringing erupted in Sami's ears.

"Oh, that hurts." Tate clapped her hands over her ears, and Fiona ran forward, her hand out as if to block the noise.

Sami fell in behind her. No way would she let her little sister face the Skaar alone.

But their progress route was cut off when a giant black dragon thudded to the ground between them and the Skaar. With a mad gleam in his blood-red eyes, Malrik smiled.

But beneath the smile was wrath. "You're mine now." Brazenly, he dismounted.

The ringing intensified, and Sami couldn't stop herself from crying out. It felt like drills were piercing her ear canals.

"Give me the ring." Malrik held out his hand.

"Die .. first," Sami managed to squeeze out.

"Fine." He laughed, but the sound held no mirth. "You can die first, and then I'll take the ring."

Voices called from somewhere, and they seemed to be getting closer. How was that possible? Were the Skaar only targeting Sami and her sisters?

"Malrik!" Rook screamed the cruel king's name, and shortly after his shout, Sami heard Grayson's.

"Get away from her, you bastard."

*Tate*, Sami sent to her sister as Malrik drew near and pulled out a knife. *Don't let him get it.*

*Sami, fight,* Tate replied.

Tears fought for release, but Sami refused to give in. Summoning all her strength, she closed her fingers to protect the ring.

"I keep my promises, witch." Malrik slid the sharp edge of his blade along Sami's arm, leaving a thin line of blood behind. "Now I'm going to peel your flesh."

"No!" Grayson was coming, but he seemed so far away.

Over the painful shrieking in her head, Sami picked up on another sound, another voice. A woman screamed, she bellowed her fury.

Malrik glanced up, his eyes rounded with shock, as a blue blur sailed over Sami and onto King Malrik.

Horrible grunts issued forth, but Sami could barely make sense of what was happening.

Hands fell to her shoulders, before sliding beneath her arms to pick her up. "Sami, talk to me."

The ringing sound was fading, and she could hear Grayson's beautiful voice. "What happened?" Sami jerked and tried to break free. "Malrik! He's right here."

"He's done," Grayson said, and Sami followed his line of sight to the rocky ground, where Malrik lay sprawled on his back.

With Hellana's blade jammed into his heart.

The daughter he so abused now stood over him with no readable emotion on her face. Rook had one arm around her, holding her steady as she swayed.

"Hold! I am the Mystic of Eirdorn." The older woman stalked across the ground as if incensed. "Stop this now. Malrik is dead!"

With the return of her strength, Sami stood fully upright and watched as the Skaar finally broke from their coordinated movements and began whispering amongst themselves.

"Your families have been freed by Queen Hellana and Lord Rook. Cease your attack." The Mystic flipped the tails of her mantle, continuing to glare at the spellcasters.

"He's really dead," Hellana said. Her unreadable expression, and her lips curved. "I'm finally free." She spun around and into Rook's arms. "We're all finally free."

Unable to accept the truth, Sami walked over to Malrik. And even though his skin had turned a dry, brittle gray, she still kicked him to be sure.

"Most of his men are dead as well." Wiping a hand on his brow, Ronan shook his sword. "And those who survived are on the run." He ran a gentle hand over Fiona's short cap of hair. "And this, my love, is my very last war."

"Good." Fiona smashed herself against him. "Now let's go make babies."

With laughter and teasing remarks all around, the core group assembled. And while it may have been morbid to assemble around Malrik's shriveling corpse, it also seemed oddly apropos.

"A feast!" Rook thrust a fist into the air. "And all are welcome, and may the spirits flow freely!"

Leaning into Grayson, Sami asked, "So what about it? Are you up for a feast?"

"Hardly seems right to deny Rook the chance to play host."

"Rook," Sami said to her friend. Her good, true, Iele friend. "What about the rest of my family? Would it be possible—"

"Arelia escorts them here as we speak. And fear not, Brit," he added with a tilt of his head, "the travel will not harm your bairn."

A loud snarl reminded them all that Malrik's vipera still sat waiting. The beast did not attack, nor did he make any aggressive move. He simply stared at the people surrounding his dead master.

Then with a shriek, he leaped into the air and flew away. The remaining dragons sounded out to each other, then fell into formation for the flight back toward the North.

"And what about you, LeRoux?" Sami stepped away but held his fingers lightly with her own. "What's next? Where do you go from here?"

"Well, there are still more offspring to be rounded up back in our world." He gave her a lopsided grin. "But I happen to know a young tracker who is eager to rise through the ranks. He'd probably be willing to step in for a while. If I asked him to."

"And will you?" Sami's throat clutched. "Will you take some time off?"

"I have about twenty years of vacation time accrued." Now he tugged her to him, her chest bumping against his. "So I think I can work something out. It might be nice to spend some time near the water, maybe find myself a bull-headed, bohemian artist to spend time with."

"Bull-headed? That's rich, coming from the man who can't take no for an answer."

"Not from you." He bent down to nuzzle her neck. "Not anymore. Just try to send me away. Try to tell me you don't love me."

"Never," she said, a strange hitch in her voice. "I'll never push you away again." She slid her hands into his silky black hair. "Come stay with me, Grayson. I want to be with you. I want to *love* you."

Around them, the Vei Lanians celebrated, and her sisters' happy voices carried on the wind. Laying her hand over his heart, Sami felt the beat in time with her own. "You and I make our own kind of magick."

With a bright Iele sun above, he brought his lips down to hers once more. But before the kiss, he whispered, "Now that's something I can believe in."

Suza Kates writes both paranormal romance and romantic suspense. She lives in Savannah, Georgia with her family and four ridiculously spoiled cats.

For more on Suza and her books visit

www.suzakates.com